# COURT OF THE FALLEN

*An Urban Fantasy*

# ANN GIMPEL

# CONTENTS

# COURT OF THE FALLEN
## MAGICK AND MISFITS SERIES, BOOK THREE

**An Urban Fantasy**

**By**
**Ann Gimpel**

**Tumble off reality's edge into a twisted world
fueled by myth and magick**

## Copyright Page

# BOOK DESCRIPTION, COURT OF THE FALLEN

**Urban fantasy and slow-burn romance wrapped into a serial that will keep you up reading long into the night.**

**Strange bedfellows rock worlds.**

Faery has changed so much I barely recognize her. I suppose every regent who loses a major war feels the same way about his country. The worst part is I didn't see this coming. A few minor skirmishes, sure, but the Unseelie fielded tens of thousands against us. The King of Winter is finally exacting revenge against the consort who spurned him. The rest of us are collateral damage. He played his hand well, attracted powerful allies, and punted us into a definite one-down position.

For the moment.

Pegasus is the king's primary ally. I possess knowledge that will blow their partnership sky high. And proof in case neither of them believes me. Timing is everything, though. Not putting my evidence in danger is at the tiptop of my list. I love Dariyah, and I wouldn't draw attention her way if it weren't necessary. She'd pooh-pooh my pussyfooting around. Even if I wanted to muffle her connection to Pegasus, she'd overrule me and throw it in his horsey face.

We must wrest Faery from the enemy. I finally hold the land link, but success is far from a foregone conclusion. More blood will flow before we're done. Buckets of the stuff, but I can't let that stop me.

BOOKS IN THE MAGICK AND
MISFITS SERIES:

AUTHOR'S NOTE:

Book covers play a big role in my creative process. I saw a set of covers featuring a badass Fae prince a while back and bid on them. Unfortunately, someone had a faster Internet connection than me, so I didn't end up with them. But everything comes out as it should because I found another cover I liked even better: the one on *Court of Rogues*, first of the Magick and Misfits books.

I've always been fascinated with the Otherworld. The faeries' ancestral home goes by many names. It's called *Annwn* in Welsh mythology and *Avalon* in Arthurian legend. In Irish mythology it's referred to as *Tír na nÓg, Mag Mell,* and *Emain Ablach.* Irish myths also feature a place called *Tech Duinn*, where the souls of the dead gather.

But I digress. My vision is a world where mortal and faery collide.

You, my readers, will let me know how well I managed it.

## CHAPTER ONE, TITANIA

Titania ducked into a quiet clearing away from the mass of injured scattered across the verdant glade of the Midnight Court. She needed a break from tending to Faery's assorted inhabitants. Most would recover, but helping a few past their pain was a final kindness. Even though it was the only reasonable path, each death seared her soul. Faery's inhabitants were immortal, but immortality only went so far. It didn't take a crystal ball or her sister's assorted scrying tools to know things weren't going especially well.

Being gone from Faery for half a century didn't help anything, but it wasn't as if she'd had a choice in the matter. Titania marshaled her practical side. She was back in Faery, and she aimed to remain there. Her fatal error had been not taking it seriously when her erstwhile consort's troops had shanghaied her. She'd been certain it was one more of his many machinations designed to exert control over her, but when weeks had passed, followed by months, the ugly truth had dawned.

Oberon wasn't coming to release her. No one was.

She'd upped the ante on her escape efforts, but Oberon had masterminded her abduction and taken more care than usual to ensure she'd be gone for good. No matter what she did, she hadn't been able to break free. Her own magic was part and parcel of her prison, woven into the stuff of the miniature castle holding her captive. When she called on her power, the walls of her prison grew stronger. When she cut its flow, she effectively crippled her ability to do anything else.

Almost back in her rightful spot, Titania didn't waste time stewing over trivialities. Dubrova Castle was where she should have been, but Ysir, the ancient Fae librarian, had just blown it sky high to keep the King of Winter and his Unseelie hordes from helping themselves to various castle treasures, including what had been a rich-and-varied collection of books and scrolls.

The library was an incalculable loss, but she couldn't stop to grieve about collected lore and wisdom that dated to the beginnings of the world.

Thank all the gods Oberon appeared to be out of the way. He'd no doubt outlived his usefulness to the King of

Winter, who'd never had any intention of sharing Faery once it fell under his control.

"There you are." Cynwrigg ap Llyr, regent of Faery, popped into view. With his tall, lithe body, ice-blond hair, and eyes like burnished metal, he was one striking man. Oberon had been beautiful, but Cynwrigg outshone him by a factor of a hundred. Dark trousers clung to his long legs, and a cream-colored linen shirt with old-fashioned bell sleeves cinched at the wrists flowed around his shoulders and torso. Scuffed leather boots graced his feet.

"Here I am." She eyed him and girded herself for whatever he wanted. He'd obviously been hunting for her, which meant he had a purpose in mind.

"I've assembled the court, my queen. By the grace of the gods, all the delegates survived. It would be good for morale if you joined us."

A corner of her mouth twisted into a sneer. "Court of the fallen, eh?"

He slitted his eyes and gripped her forearm. Before she could twist away and rebuke him for touching her, he said, "Our situation is temporary. Snide commentary like that won't help any of us."

She did jerk her arm out of his grip. "Now look here. Calling a spade a spade is honest. We have to tack down a starting point, if we're going to develop plans that have any hope of success."

The stark set to Cynwrigg's features softened slightly. "Every one of Faery's citizens is all too aware we lost the battle despite our best efforts. Most know Ysir leveled Dubrova. The explosion sent shock waves through the land. Coming up with a label that memorializes our failure isn't helpful."

Anger moved from a simmer to a slow boil. How dare he tell her the right way to treat with her subjects. Hers, not his. "I was queen long before you were born, and—"

"Your point?" he cut her off rudely.

"You could be replaced," she sputtered, expecting him to fold.

"All right by me," he shot back. "I never wanted to be regent, and I still don't, but I will uphold my duty to the land and to you." Breath swished from between his teeth. "Come join the court. They can vote someone else into my slot."

"I heard some of that." Auril bustled into the clearing. What had felt like plenty of space for one was growing crowded. Her sister's long, lush red hair hung in tangles to her waist. Smudges of dirt and blood tracked down her face and coated her hands. Auril's silver eyes bored into her and Cynwrigg as she glanced from one to the other of them. Auril had always been tall. Not quite up to Cynwrigg's seven-foot height, but not far from it, either. A dark-blue skirt hung off her hips, and she wore a black blouse and a leather vest with a million little pockets stuffed with healing powders, potions, and crystals. As usual, her feet were bare.

"You were eavesdropping, so what?" Titania countered.

*"Our people are understandably shaken."* Auril switched to mind speech. *"We must present a united front and shore them up. If we do not, they won't have the heart for the series of battles I've seen in my pool."*

"I thought you didn't have a clear picture of what comes next," Cynwrigg said.

Auril nodded. "I didn't, but I've taken the odd break here and there and looked. The future has a way of showing itself to me in its own time, and—"

"Do we win?" Titania cut her sister off. She wasn't interested in fluff, only in results.

Auril skewered her with an annoyed expression. "Eventually. If we don't make any more mistakes."

"I wasn't even here," Titania reminded her. "So, if there were errors..." She quit talking. She'd just been replaying her serious lapse in judgement not pulling out every weapon in her arsenal to fight off Oberon's henchmen fifty years before. Her statement about none of this being her fault died unspoken.

"If there were errors, then what?" Auril asked sweetly.

"Never mind." Titania snapped her jaws firmly shut

before she stuffed her foot so far into her mouth a sandal emerged from her ass.

"I'm going to greet the court," Cynwrigg said. "I would very much appreciate both of you being there." Turning on his heel, he left without another word. He'd taken the wind out of her sails with his proclamation he'd be delighted to step down as regent. Since he didn't care about the position, it didn't leave her much leverage. Or any at all.

Auril dropped a hand onto her shoulder. "We're not at our best, none of us—" she began.

"Stuff it."

The hand gripping her shoulder tightened almost to the point of pain. "Sister," Auril hissed, "no one is pleased by today's outcome. If we don't get lost squabbling among ourselves, we might pull out of the hole we've dug ourselves into."

Titania straightened her back. "We did not do this to ourselves. We were the victims of a nefarious scheme that trapped us in its maw."

"Wrong answer. We only turn into victims when we feel sorry for ourselves. Goddammit, Titania, draw yourself together. Be Faery's queen, not some simpering ninny running around proclaiming the sky has fallen."

"I resent that." She sent a short blast of magic designed to make Auril let go, but her sister clung like a stubborn limpet. "The sky did fall. Faery is heading into her endgame."

Auril switched things up and drew back a hand. For a moment Titania thought her sister was going to slap her. It wouldn't be the first time, but Auril dropped her arm to her side and growled, "Desperate straits, yes. Endgame suggests a point of no return, and we are not out of choices. Not yet. I'm going to join the court. I suggest you get past whatever is eating you alive and do the same."

Titania stared after Auril's retreating form. Back in the day, no one in Faery would have dared address her in such a manner, sister or no. Oberon had meted out punishment for insubordination and—

"Aye, and he's gone," she muttered. "I was only the queen, the consort. No one took me seriously." Titania swallowed hard. Truth was a bitter draught, but important to face. She had an opportunity to establish herself as Faery's remaining royalty in more than name, and she wouldn't do it with negativity. It didn't matter whose fault today was.

What was critical was what they did about it. When she wasn't so pissed, she'd thank Auril for a timely boot in the butt. For now, she hurried out of the place she'd hoped for a respite—and hadn't found one—to the rows of wounded. Work awaited. She'd do a spot more healing, and then drop in on the court.

A unicorn cantered up to her. "You're needed at the north end of the glade, my queen. More of your subjects are fading."

The pair of satyrs she'd been summoned to help both made it. Auril's daughter, Dariyah, had knelt by her side, mixing magics with hers, which speeded up the process considerably. The woman was a powerhouse. Titania's understanding of why her sister had insisted on heeding the call of fortune and mating with Pegasus came into true focus for the first time. When they'd finished with the satyrs, Dariyah rocked back on her heels and said, "That went well, Auntie."

Titania nodded. "Our enchantments blend nicely."

"They should." Dariyah grinned. "Blood knows its own and all that goes with it. I'm going to clean up and join the court."

"As am I. If anyone asks, tell them I'll be there soon." She hadn't realized those were her intentions until the words slipped out, but she'd wait a few more minutes before leaving the impromptu field hospital. Something about healing, where she drew the strands of body and soul back together, had a centering effect. After two more successful interventions—and one death—she pushed to her feet and headed to where she assumed Cynwrigg had assembled the court.

Sure enough, they were arranged around the altar Auril used to convene the Midnight Court. Cynwrigg spied her immediately and gestured her forward. As if she required an invitation.

*Stop. Just stop,* her caustic inner critic sniped. *Be one with your people. It's the only way.*

After her last interaction with Cynwrigg, he could just as well have ignored her. Except he wouldn't have done that. He wasn't being polite; he was laying the foundations to restore Faery's confidence. He'd been frank concerning how he felt about being regent. Regardless, he was putting Faery first, above his personal wishes.

If he could manage it, by the goddess so could she.

"Thank you," she said and nodded his way before turning to the dozen court delegates, Ysir, Auril, and Dariyah. The Fae librarian had changed. He no longer looked like a doddering old man. In his place stood a warrior, harsh and resolute.

"The wounded required my presence. It is why I was late," she told the group.

No reason to mention she'd needed time to become the queen they deserved.

"Please. Tell me what ground you've covered," she went on. "What's been decided, and what remains to be hammered out?"

Auril rose to her feet. "Mostly, I've been doing my damnedest to home in on the immediate future."

"You said you'd seen parts of it. What grew clearer?"

Titania crooked two fingers her sister's way while marveling once again how much she and Dariyah resembled one another. More like twins than mother and daughter with their red hair, statuesque bearing, and strong facial structure.

"We require assistance. No matter how I spin the elements, there is no way we can wrest our land back without help."

"Will the dragons be sufficient?" Titania arched a brow.

Auril shook her head. "They might have been if Pegasus and that mother of his weren't involved."

"But they're only two," Titania protested. "Surely we can neutralize them."

"Not only two," Auril corrected her. "That would be simpler. Medusa is one of three Gorgons. Stheno and Euryale are her sisters. Unlike Medusa, they are truly immortal. Medusa had to jump through hoops to come back to life after Perseus chopped off her head."

"Keep going," Titania urged. She knew Auril well enough to understand there was more.

"Aye. Medusa birthed another monster beyond Pegasus. Chrysaor is a giant, loyal to Pegasus, and very much a power to be reckoned with. And then there are the Shadow Lords. I am not certain of their involvement, but we must ready ourselves in case they play a part of this." Auril pursed her mouth into a sour expression.

"There was never anything wrong with the King of Winter's mental capacities. He chose his allies well."

He had, indeed. If anyone would know, Auril would since she'd spent centuries as his consort before finally turning on her heel and walking away. Titania took in the court delegates. They didn't appear as devastated as she'd figured they would be.

"Chrysaor is a winged wild boar if I remember properly," she muttered.

"Some legends depict him as a mighty warrior wielding a golden blade," Cynwrigg tossed out.

"Not sure it matters," Auril said. "Chrysaor can select which form he presents. Both are deadly. But it isn't those arrayed against us so much as how their magic slots together. What I'd begun to say was we require intervention from those more powerful than us."

Titania didn't like the sound of that. Auril must be referring to the gods, and they'd never been particularly accommodating. Her only interactions with them had ended up with her retreating, tail between her legs and swearing she'd never put herself in that position again.

*Eh. Never is a long time.*

"What exactly did your scrying reveal, Sister?"

"It doesn't work that way, and you know as much," Auril replied. "I have seen battles replay themselves many ways, but all with the same ending. We lose again. Unless something major changes."

"Were dragons fighting alongside us?"

"Aye, they were. It dragged the fighting out, but the results were the same. Three Gorgons and two monsters, a Shadow Lord lurking on the sidelines, plus all those Unseelie, were too much. Now if we could send the Unseelie battalions back to wherever they came from—"

"Did we ever figure out where their portal led?" Cynwrigg broke in.

One of the unicorn delegates whinnied. "No. The dragons closed the gateway. Perhaps if we'd examined it sooner, we'd have discovered something. As it was, when we looked more closely, magic bounced back at us."

"They must have a staging area on some other world," Titania said.

"I suggested much the same," Dariyah chimed in. "Even offered to hunt for it."

Titania rolled her shoulders back and wished for her sister's height. Hell, she wished for a lot of things. Her scepter. Her cozy rooms in Dubrova. She had to forget any of them had ever existed.

"I will be forthright with you," she said, "calling in any of the gods is my last choice. Not that we can't do it if nothing else works, but they've never guaranteed much of anything except strife. Getting them to agree on a direction that meshes with our needs would be our first challenge. Even if they did, they'll have their own agendas. And they won't tell us about them until it comes time to pay the piper for their help. We may not care for the price, but by then it will be too late to quibble."

She shrugged. "We could attempt to clarify details at the front end, but if it's in their best interest to keep us in the dark, it's exactly what they'll do."

"Sounds like you've had direct experience," Cynwrigg observed.

"I have." She stopped there, unwilling to vomit up her humiliation at the hands of the gods. Oberon had sent her on several junkets until she'd refused to be his errand girl anymore.

Ysir pushed upright. "If I may, my queen."

"Certainly," she replied.

"The way I see it"—Ysir walked until he stood next to her and Cynwrigg facing the group—"our first task is to locate the place the Unseelie are congregating and destroy it. It won't make a dent in the bunch ranged around what used to be Dubrova, but at least it will cut down on having to deal with more of them.

"While some of us are working on that project, others can research the magic standing against us." His lined face crinkled into a Cheshire cat grin. "I made a good show of blowing up the castle, but I preserved most of the library. No one will wade through the wreckage looking for it, but that cuts both ways. We will have trouble accessing the materials too."

Titania felt like cheering. Loss of the library had dealt them a crippling blow, except it wasn't gone after all.

Cynwrigg clapped Ysir across the shoulders. "You should consider a career on stage. I believed you when you said a librarian needed a library and you'd obliterated yours."

Ysir's smile widened. "'Twasn't too far off the mark. Everything around it was annihilated."

"Good man. Thanks for not following my instructions."

Ysir turned to Cynwrigg. "Not a problem, Regent. It's good you're not wedded to being in charge. Had you been, you might have minded me picking a different road."

"Not at all." Cynwrigg shook his cascade of pale hair behind his shoulders. "I felt like a bastard sending you off to destroy the history of our people, but the alternative felt worse."

"I understand. I bought us the best of both worlds. We shall see how things play out."

"Who will search out the Unseelie lair?" Titania projected her voice until she hoped it smacked of command.

"Dariyah and I will take a crack at it," Cynwrigg said.

"And I will creep into the library and gather what information I can about the Gorgons, Shadow Lords, Pegasus, and Chrysaor," Ysir said.

"It's a solid start," Titania said. "The rest of us will shore up Faery's citizens. Some will require time before they're fully themselves again. Meanwhile, take the healthy and form companies. Practice battle techniques every day. We didn't start with a country of warriors, but there's no reason why we can't build one."

Cheers rang out, startling her. What she'd said hadn't been all that inspiring. Or maybe it had. She wasn't in a position to judge.

Auril joined her. "Might I add an item or two?"

"Of course."

"I will continue to scry our future at every opportunity," Auril told the group. "I will also reconvene the Midnight Court. It will help us heal." She turned to Titania. "How often would you like us to touch base?"

Titania smothered a grimace. Auril was subtlety reminding her what she'd left out. "Let's reconvene two afternoons hence at about this same time. If you miss a meeting or two because you're not here, find me on your return and I can let you know how we're doing as we move forward.

"And we will move forward," she went on. "Faery suffered a monumental loss today, but we are not done for. We will rise above this. We will reclaim our land."

When the shouting and clapping had died down, she turned to Cynwrigg. "Before you leave, check in with the land."

"Aye, my queen. I'd planned to do just that."

"Does anyone have any questions? Ideas? Things we missed today?" Titania let her gaze settle on each delegate in turn. She knew them all, and a more solid bunch of mages didn't exist in all of Faery.

No one said anything, so she went on, "As you go about your tasks, things will come to you. Write them down and bring them to the next meeting."

Amid a sea of yesses and ayes, the group disbanded. Titania turned to go too, but Auril grabbed her arm. "Nicely done."

She turned to her sister and lowered her voice. "Thanks."

"None needed. You know me. I never lavish praise when it hasn't been earned."

"You're not kidding," Dariyah snarked and then laughed.

Leaving them to tease one another, Titania walked toward Auril's modest cottage. Today had gone better than she'd expected. Not only had she instilled hope in the court delegates, she actually believed her own hype. Things weren't as desperate as she'd painted them.

Faery had a hard road ahead, but she was queen of these lands and she'd see things through. Not having to sit in Oberon's shadow and forever worry about his moods was an incredible boon. She'd make mistakes, but she'd recover from them.

"Aye," she murmured to herself, "a queen who never blunders isn't doing enough, isn't taking chances, isn't being the best possible leader for her people."

She passed beneath the lintel of Auril's home and poured herself a tumblerful of mead, sighing as the spicy heat of it passed down her throat. She'd earned an hour or two to herself, but then she'd be back in the thick of things.

*"Sister."* Auril's telepathy held sharp edges. *"You're needed now."*

Titania drained the rest of her glass. Maybe it was a good thing she hadn't sat down. *"Where?"*

*"The eastern border of the Midnight Court. We caught two Unseelie, and—"*

*"Interrogate them,"* Titania ordered.

*"Too late. They're dead, but this means they've found us."*

*"Maybe. Maybe not. On my way."*

She bolted from the house and took off running. It was almost as fast as a teleport spell, and the movement helped clear her mind. It was possible the Unseelie hadn't yet reported in. It was also possible they'd wandered into Auril's lands accidentally. The Midnight Court cast a seductive allure, drawing all things magical.

She'd issue blanket orders that all spies were to be

tortured until they talked. It was messier than killing outright, but war was messy business. Brutalizing the Unseelie held a certain appeal. More than an appeal. She was looking forward to jabbing and prodding and cutting off body parts.

The coppery smell of fresh blood made her alter course. She bounded into a thicket and found Auril, a unicorn, and a couple of nymphs standing over the corpses. "Cut off their right hands and have the birds drop them into the middle of the Unseelie camp."

Auril grinned. "Why, Sister. What a splendid idea."

"Forcing them to talk would have been even more 'splendid,'" she retorted.

"Agreed." The unicorn pawed the ground. "I gored them. Next time, I shall exercise restraint."

She patted his flank. "I know you will. Get to it."

## CHAPTER TWO, CYN

"Still want dinner at Lady Luck?" I asked Dariyah.

"You know I do." She grinned up at me, and my heart took flight. Gods but she was gorgeous. Her green eyes glowed like exotic gems. Today they'd taken on mossy overtones with golden flecks around her pupils.

"I was sorting logistics," she said. "How about this for a plan? I'll make certain no more of the wounded require tending to. Once I'm done here, I'll look in on Midnight and then head for the casino."

"Is that a diplomatic way of avoiding coming to see Faery with me?"

Her smile faded. "Maybe not so much diplomatic as practical. She's furious with me for refusing to cede my body to her needs." Dariyah shook her head until tangled red hair swirled around her shoulders. "After that last time when she took one look at Medusa and exited stage left, I made up my mind. She can find some other body to borrow when she feels the need."

"She can hear you," I cautioned.

"Yeah. I know, but I'm not telling her anything new. Eh, maybe if she admitted what she'd done, rather than rewriting history, I'd reconsider."

I gripped one of her hands, lacing my fingers with hers. "Sharing your physical form again is far too risky. Once she's part of you, the only reason she relinquishes her hold is because she wants to. With the land in desperate straits, she'll have many reasons to cling to corporeality."

"Until there's nothing left of me," Dariyah mumbled. "I get it." Angling her head to one side, she frowned. "Say. So long as Ysir is making a library run, could he maybe hunt down information about Faery. Did she have a body once? If she did, what happened to it?"

"I'm sure he already knows. But you can ask him. Or I could."

A small bump of magic jostled me: Dariyah's mind voice reaching out for Ysir. His reply didn't surprise me. *"I already know both answers. I'll find you once I've returned."*

*"Cyn and I won't be here,"* Dariyah reminded him.

*"No matter. Next time our paths cross is soon enough."*

Dariyah leaned into me, and then released my hand. "I should run. As long as I'm stopping by my flat, I'll clean up."

"Why not bring Midnight along to Lady Luck," I suggested.

"The cat's not fond of teleporting," she reminded me. "But I'll see if he's up for a short jaunt. Bye. See you soon." She blew an air kiss my way.

I blew one back, feeling silly, and walked away from the Midnight Court, past the barrier separating it from the rest of Faery. Something about Ysir's words nagged at me, but the associated memories wouldn't cooperate. Faery had been corporeal once. What had happened to alter that?

*"Ysir?"*

*"Aye, Regent."*

*"How did Faery lose access to her body?"*

*"Oberon found it inconvenient when she challenged him, so he cast a spell to force her to adopt her current form."*

*"Can it be undone?"* I asked. If Faery had her own body, maybe her anger at Dariyah would dissipate.

*"I do not know, but I will look. Apologies, but I should hold silence. The less magic expended, the safer."*

I cut the connection—no reason to add to his risk apologizing—and set a path for Faery's foundations. I'd expected her to be hounding me about Dubrova, but she hadn't said a word. If the castle's demolition bothered her, I hadn't felt anything through our link.

Faery wasn't shy about voicing disapproval. She'd made her antipathy clear the last time I'd held Dariyah in my arms. What had she said? Something like, "Not her. Anyone but her."

I'd given the land my word I'd relinquish my link to her if she requested it of me. More than my word, I'd sealed the vow with a blood bond. It removed the element of choice from the equation. It was remotely possible Faery would get so spun out about Dariyah, she'd tell me she was done, but the alternatives who'd move into my vacated spot weren't especially desirable.

By now, the King of Winter must know I was linked with the land. He was like as not plotting to unseat me. The quickest path was by separating me from my magic. It would spell certain death.

Blowing out a tense breath, I stopped moving long enough to clear my head. I didn't want to spend much time beneath Faery. Only long enough to reassure the land we weren't going to give up on her. She'd know as much, anyway, because she was privy to all my thoughts —if she chose to look.

Gathering power around me, I borrowed liberally from Faery as I sank through her varied layers, ending up in a cave studded with crystals that reflected the entire spectrum of light. One spot glowed brighter, and I aimed my words at it.

"I am sorry about the castle, but—"

*"Pfft. I never cared for it."*

I'd always been taught its foundations were mingled with the land. How much else of what was fed to us in mage school had been incorrect?

I cleared my throat. "The court—and everyone else —has moved to the portion of Faery Auril carved out for herself, and—"

*"Regent. If you showed up to provide a running commentary about how Faery is doing, save your breath. I already know."*

Her attitude was pissing me off. I almost missed the days when we'd had to communicate using falling stones rather than words. "How about this topic?" I suggested sweetly. "Ysir tells me the reason you're separated from your body is because of something Oberon did. Is there any action on my part that would help restore you to wholeness?"

*"Aye. Give me Dariyah. It will solve multiple...problems."*

"Not going to happen." I'd have added I was in love with her and hoped she'd be my mate one day, but Faery already knew as much. "I need to leave for a while. Part of my task is locating the Unseelie's staging area. It must be on another world, so I will be gone for a while. For now, consider my offer. Surely between my magic—and Dariyah's that complements it—we can break through Oberon's spell."

*"I will think about it."*

It was better than an out-and-out no. Always wise to leave on a high note, so I turned and retraced my steps, half expecting her to order me back. She didn't. As I made my way to a spot where it wouldn't require much magic to teleport to Earth, I thought about Oberon's spell. That it was still active meant he had to be alive somewhere.

The simplest way out for Faery would be for someone—preferably me—to end the old geezer forever, but I had other fish to fry. The stairs below Lady Luck took shape around me, and I walked up them. My original reason for buying this establishment and running it had been to give me an easy cover to come and go on Earth while I searched for a rift beneath Faery.

Dariyah had not only found the breach, she'd also cured it. Since the casino had outlived its usefulness, I should sell the place. It was obscenely profitable, so locating a buyer wouldn't be difficult. When I'd purchased it, it had been sucking fumes, but I'd turned it around.

Not a decision I had to make today. I did a walk through on the way to my office on the top floor. Lady

Luck was huge. Over sixty thousand square feet spread over four floors. The place had every type of gaming imaginable including virtual horseracing. We ran a mostly invisible string of call girls—and boys—with a discreet madam managing them. Everything seemed to be running smoothly, but the night was young. If things were going to get sticky, the shit didn't usually hit the fan till past midnight.

I unlocked my office with a small shot of magic and went to work catching up on my neglected bookkeeping. So much of the money that ran through Lady Luck was dirty, I felt compelled to maintain the appearance of an honest establishment. Not that my place was different from any of the large casinos in Reno. They're all crooked as a dog's hind leg.

There's an association of casino managers. They'd nagged me to join for years, but I came up with enough excuses they finally left me alone. I didn't need to be any closer than I already was to organized crime syndicates.

I felt Dariyah's magic before she walked through a hole in the air with a large black cat yowling in her arms. "There, silly. We're here," she informed the cat. "Told you it would be quick."

"Mrrrrooowwwwww."

She set Midnight on the floor. He leapt through the air and ended up dead center on my desk, hissing. Before he shredded my pile system, I doused him with catnip fumes laced into a calming infusion.

Dariyah laughed. "He won't rest until he finds the catnip."

"How about a virtual bush?" I suggested.

"It will work until he tries to destroy it with his claws. How'd it go with Faery?"

"All right. She requested you as a permanent sacrifice. I refused."

A snort rolled from Dariyah. "Gosh. Thanks. Where do I leave my contribution for your generosity."

I got up, came around the desk, and folded her into my arms. Meanwhile, the cat had jumped down and was busily sniffing every corner of my office, certain if he turned over enough stones, he'd locate the catnip.

"I'm cheap," I told her. "I work for kisses."

The shock as our mouths connected started in my toes and raced through me like fine old whiskey, warm and alluring. Dariyah is tall for a woman, and our bodies fit together like they were made for each other. She opened to my kiss, and I teased the inside of her mouth with my tongue. The peaks of her breasts hardened against my chest, and my cock swelled to fullness. My fingertips played over damp hair and soft skin.

I raised my mouth from hers. "You smell divine."

"Cheap coconut shampoo, but thanks. Did you order dinner?"

I'd been rocking against her, food the last thing on my mind. "I was waiting to see what you wanted."

"Liar." She laughed, and the sound tickled my ears. After what we'd lived through, I'd wondered if laughter had departed from the world.

"You're right. I fell down a rabbit hole wondering if I should sell this place and moved from there to the accounting that keeps it floating."

She drew her red brows together and kneaded my shoulders with her strong hands. "Do you need to sell it? I mean, is it going broke or something?"

I shook my head. "Nothing could be further from the truth. My only reason for being here was the rift, though."

"I think you should keep it," she said firmly. "Hard to know how things are going to shake out in Faery. We might need a fallback position." She wriggled out of my arms. "If I stay smushed up against you, we'll never get to eating, and..."

"Were you always a taskmistress?" My groin throbbed. The front of my trousers was tented like a sail in a staunch gale.

"Try being raised by Auril. She wrote the book on taskmistress-ness. I used to tease her about being a dominatrix without a sub to push around."

My turn to laugh, and I did uproariously. The vision of Auril in leather, whip in hand, was hilarious. In betwixt and between, I managed to order us up a meal from the kitchen.

"What else did Faery have to say?" Dariyah asked after moving Midnight away from the drapes he'd been chewing a hole through.

"Your questions to Ysir made me think," I replied. "Faery did have a body once. What I couldn't remember was how she'd lost it, so I raised the librarian and asked him."

"Oh?" Dariyah arched her brows.

"Aye. According to Ysir, Oberon got sick of Faery going toe-to-toe with him, so he separated her from her body."

"But surely we can fix that," she said excitedly. "When she has her own body, she won't be jonesing for mine."

"Same thing I'd thought," I replied, "but when I offered to help find a way to reclaim it, she didn't exactly jump on the opportunity."

"That's odd. I wonder why not?"

"What I questioned was why the spell was still active," I retorted. "It has to mean Oberon is alive somewhere."

Dariyah snapped her fingers. "Exactly. All we have to do is find him and kill him for good. And then everything he crafted with magic will fall apart." She nodded enthusiastically. "I like it. Let's slot it in somewhere after finding the Unseelies and returning to Faery."

"Mmph. Auril was part drill sergeant too, huh?"

"Damn. I feel like my underwear is showing."

A knock sounded at the door followed by one of the kitchen staff rolling a tray. I hadn't realized I was hungry until the smells of roasted meat, potatoes, and salad hit me, and then my mouth started to water.

Midnight leapt through the air and landed in the middle of the serving tray. Dariyah shooed him off. "There's plenty to share," I told her and filched a bowl from the cupboard above my small refrigerator. So long as I was there, I asked what she wanted to drink.

"Whatever you're having is fine," she replied.

After skimming off a few choice bits of meat for the cat, I settled across from Dariyah. For the next few minutes we inhaled the tri-tip and garlicy twice-baked potatoes. The salad was perfect. Crisp romaine with just the right amount of Caesar dressing and crumbly croutons.

"I could get used to this." Dariyah set down her fork. "Erm. Do you ever cook?"

"Not often." I smiled. "But I know how. It's impossible to live as long as I have and not pick up a few survival skills."

"Maybe the kitchen is one more reason not to sell this place." She drained what was left of her mineral water and angled her head to one side. "Any ideas where to start looking for the Unseelies?"

"Nary a one." A glance at my plate told me I'd cleared it down to the ceramic. "Titania appears to have had some less than pleasant run-ins with the gods, but perhaps we could scare one up. They might know something."

"Do we have other options?" Midnight jumped into her lap and proceeded to lick her empty plate.

I shrugged. "Sure. We can start searching worlds one by one, but it could take years without any clues."

"Even if we locate them"—Dariyah paused long enough to take a measured breath—"this is a reconnaissance, right? Two of us wouldn't be much of a match for however many thousands of Unseelie there are."

"I'd hoped to solicit aid from the dragons, but first we have to see what's out there. So, yes, a reconnaissance."

Dariyah chewed on her lower lip. "I have another idea, but it's risky."

"Go on," I urged. Nothing these days was risk-free.

"The unicorn said they'd failed to follow the pathway after dragons shut the Unseelies' portal. Maybe they didn't look deep enough."

"What do you mean?"

"I'm certain they applied standard tracking magic,"

Dariyah went on. "It ran into a wall or bounced back at them, and they quit. What if we pushed it. Hard."

We were incredibly strong when we joined forces. It was definitely worth a shot. "I like it," I said. "If it works, it will save a lot of time. I'm not seeing the dicey aspect, though."

"We could get stuck. Once the Unseelie understood we were onto them, they must have altered the passageway on their end too. So even if we manage to blow through whatever the dragons did to seal it, we could run into a different set of problems."

"The other end is probably heavily guarded," I speculated.

"Or at least ringed with magical markers that will ping their silly heads off if anyone who isn't Unseelie moves within range."

"We might be able to craft an illusion," I suggested.

"What was in that beer?" she shot back. "No magic alive can alter us enough to pass for Unseelie."

Reaching across the table, I gripped her hand. All levity fled when I said, "Not Unseelie, but you can channel your father's magic. It's pervasive enough, the Unseelie might not dig deeper."

"But if they look for him, he won't be there."

"No one will," I said. "We'll be cloaked to the nines with just enough of Pegasus's energy leaking around the edges to grease the skids."

"I've never done anything like that. I'll have to drill down and figure out what belongs to him." She unlaced her fingers from mine and got to her feet. After she was upright, she paced in a tight circle.

I stood too. "It doesn't have to be perfect. And it doesn't need to last very long. All it needs to do is cover us while we move past the portal's other end so we can take a peek around. Dariyah. Look at me."

When she did, I added, "It was only a suggestion. We don't have to do it. Or perhaps it could be a fallback position. We'll hunt for one of the gods first. If that doesn't pan out, we can go with plan B."

She creased her forehead into a mass of lines. "How many of the other worlds are easily habitable?"

"I don't know. When we sat with Ysir, he indicted only two, but we've been to three. Four if you count the one where you grew up."

"Maybe we could check them first. While we're doing that, I'll work on sorting Pegasus's magic from the rest of mine."

"Sure. Good idea. I can't see Oberon and the Lord of Winter scattering their troops too widely. Perhaps we'll get lucky and find the Unseelie in the same place we rescued Titania."

"I didn't sense any other mages beyond her guards," Dariyah murmured. "Hell, we couldn't even sense the queen because of the runes on the door, and—"

I snapped my fingers. "Got it. We'll toss neutralizing spells all over the place. We can reconstruct whatever you did to deactivate the runes."

She snorted. "Not sure about 'all over the place.' Nothing like announcing our presence with klaxons. But we can accomplish a lot with subtlety."

I piled plates back onto the cart, working around the cat. "I'll take him back to my flat," Dariyah said.

"I'll come with you, and we'll leave from there."

Midnight yowled and hissed as I draped a teleport spell around us. He didn't care for the touch of magic, and mine probably felt worse than Dariyah's. She was mother and friend, where I was a Johnny-come-lately."

Was hunting the Unseelie on our own a mistake? Potential pitfalls taunted me, but none of the other alternatives were viable. We couldn't schlepp an entire company of mages across universes to locate them. We could split up and hunt individually, but we were better off sticking together.

"Cyn?" Dariyah nudged me.

"Aye?" We stood in the middle of her mostly empty living room. She'd made some progress putting away the welter of things that had littered the center of the floor.

"Are we doing this, or not?"

I was growing used to her living in my head, sifting through my thoughts, and I welcomed her presence. "What do you think?" I tossed the ball her way.

Her mouth formed a lopsided grin. "We wing it. Write the rules as we go."

"Good enough for me."

The cat was hunched over his kibble dish when I threaded my arms around Dariyah, gathered the edges of the teleport spell I hadn't totally abandoned, and set a course for the world where we'd located Faery's queen.

3

# CHAPTER THREE, DARIYAH

I looped my magic in with Cyn's so the journey spell would go faster. Something about the traveling medium isn't comfortable, but it is convenient. Sort of a combo between beam-me-up-Scotty and having a wizened crone wave a magic wand after cackling about tradeoffs.

I'd enjoyed supper in Cyn's office. We'd had enough meals there, it was starting to feel like a second home for me. I'd hustled us along because staying wasn't wise, not the way I felt about him. Every time he touched me, my soul caught fire, and not ripping off his clothes turned into a pitched battle. One of these days we'd have more than stolen kisses and climaxes that happened because we were both so desperate for one another they forced their way out.

No matter how many times he kissed me, touched me, I longed for more. On the rare occasions when I shut my eyes for a moment, visions of him naked and straddling me, with his fair hair falling all around, rose unbidden.

"Mmmm," he murmured. "Two can jump on the mind-sharing choo-choo. I especially liked that last set of images."

I glanced up at him and winked. There was just enough light in the journey corridor for him to see. "Me too. Maybe someday."

He slid a hand down my arm until he tucked his fingers in with mine. "Definitely someday."

"How much farther?" I asked to take my mind off all the ways I wanted to make him mine. I'd already had him in my mouth, but it left about a million other things we hadn't done.

He turned to face me. His arms were still around me, and the swell of his erection prodded my belly. "That's not helping," I murmured but couldn't bring myself to wriggle out of his embrace.

"No, but you feel too good to let go of. You might start building one of those bombproof wards."

I grabbed a few strands of loose magic and looped them together. While I was at it, I remembered my plan to start sorting what part of my power belonged to the winged horse. I'd be damned if I could bring myself to call him Father.

"There," I said. "Ready for most anything."

"Good because we're nearly there."

Once he said it, I noted the edges of his spell were lighter than they'd been. I hadn't noticed because I was busy with my own tasks. The world where we'd pulled Titania from an enchanted castle jolted into view around us. Cinder heaps—all that was left of the guards we'd killed on our last trip here—smudged the landscape.

Casting spells through an effective ward has drawbacks. I did my damnedest to hunt for anything radiating magic but couldn't sense other mages. Of course, I hadn't known where Titania was, either. Cyn walked the perimeter of the clearing where Titania's guards had attacked us. They'd been Oberon's men, but they'd hardly been at their best. He'd culled troops from the *Dreaming* to compensate for no longer having a link to Faery's citizens.

Back by my side, Cyn asked, "Well?"

I shook my head and gestured we should get moving. Titania had been hidden behind illusion. Maybe she wasn't the only hidden element in this place. I didn't recall birds or small animals from our last visit, but they were here now. Lots of them.

Witches and Fae could use them as spies. It wasn't a

talent I'd ever cultivated. "Can you ask the animals?" I quirked a brow at Cyn.

"Let's look around a little first. Let them get used to us and decide we're not a threat."

"But we're warded."

"Aye, and they can still sense something is different even if they can't see us."

It was diplomatic of him. They'd never view him as a concern, but I was a different story with my mixed blood. We struck out in a northerly direction walking through woods and more open areas. Two of the raptors followed us. Interesting. I hadn't totally believed Cyn when he'd said they sensed alterations in the status quo. Other mages can't pierce my warding, but apparently the two hawks could. At least to the extent they recognized something different was present; something they wanted to keep tabs on.

"Where was Titania held?" I asked.

"We're not quite there yet."

"How come you know that, but I have to ask?"

The place our magics were joined snugged tighter. "Look there," he said. "And there."

Sure enough. When I borrowed liberally from him, bits of Titania's essence floated in the air and skimmed the ground. The queen had spent a long time here and expended gobs of magic trying to escape. The laws of physics apply to magic in that once it's been created, it can't be destroyed, merely reapportioned.

We were moving slower now. Even so, I nearly stumbled into the hole where the castle was. Jumping down, I kindled a mage light and sucked in a surprised breath. The rune-pocked doors lay at odd angles, but the structure they'd slotted into was gone. "What in the unholy hell?" I mumbled and walked around where it had stood.

"Titania's magic was part of what kept it standing. Absent her presence, it was bound to fail."

I thought about it. "Doesn't help Oberon's somewhere in the wind."

"He's probably a prisoner." Cyn's tone was matter-of-fact, yet I heard satisfaction beneath the words.

"Maybe we'll find him along with the Unseelie. Two for the price of one."

"Keep the optimism flowing. Looking as if we'll need it," Cyn muttered.

"I'll do my best. No reason to tarry." I fashioned a twist of magic to help me jump out of the chasm. When Oberon had been hot on my trail, one of my worries was he'd dump me in Titania's recently vacated prison. I was delighted it had disappeared, resorbed back into the earth it had drawn its essence from. The red-tailed hawks that had been shadowing us perched in a nearby tree.

Cyn joined me. Holding out an arm, he invited a bird

to perch on it. After quite a hesitation—during which I relaxed the warding shielding us—the larger of the pair winged toward us and wrapped his talons around Cyn's forearm.

*"The lady who lived here. Is she safe?"* the bird chirruped.

"Aye," Cyn replied. "The lady is queen of Faery, and she is safely returned. Thank you for your concern."

*"Who are you?"* the other bird flew near, but chose to circle rather than land.

"Cynwrigg ap Llyr, Regent to Faery." He inclined his head.

"And I am Dariyah," I told them.

The bird on Cyn's arm skewered me with his beady avian eyes. *"What are you, Dariyah?"*

The sixty-four thousand dollar question, eh? The bird was canny enough to understand I wasn't the Witch I appeared. The hawk must have been exposed to mages, or he'd never have recognized I wasn't what I appeared to be. How many magical beings lived here? What types? I wanted to ask, but it would be rude to answer a question with another unrelated one.

I needed to say something. The longer I put off answering, the dodgier my reply was sure to feel. "I am half Fae," I told the hawk.

"The other half of her parentage was a recent and unpleasant surprise," Cyn cut in smoothly. "It upsets her to talk about it, and perhaps it's not safe. With the queen and her guards gone, are we the only ones with magic on this world?"

The birds exchanged glances. If I didn't know better, I'd have been certain they were communicating in some telepathic form.

*"We do not want more magic people here,"* the bird on Cyn's arm said firmly.

"I understand. Dariyah and I are only here to look."

*"More of you will come, though,"* the bird in the air said.

*"And then our lands will no longer be safe for our nestlings,"* the other added and launched himself off Cyn's arm.

Cyn straightened his back, standing tall. "If the Unseelie are here, they will strip your lands bare. They care not for anything in the natural world. Laying low and hoping they leave isn't a viable strategy."

*"We cannot fight them,"* one of the birds said.

"We can," I said. "They're holding our world hostage. We must reclaim it, but first we must ensure no more of them show up."

Amid a flurry of squawking, the hawks rose high into the air and flew away, their dark wings cutting through the air.

"That's unfortunate." Cyn blew out a breath.

"Do you know what scared them off?" I asked and tugged my partially discarded ward back into place.

He shook his head and tossed power in a wide net. I followed the lines of it, searching for something magical that might be lurking. One spot felt...odd. I directed our joined magic toward it. "It's subtle, but the warp and weft of the air currents feel off," I murmured. "What do you think?"

"Whatever that is, it was here when we freed Titania. I didn't pay it any heed then."

"So that's not what lit a fire under the birds?"

"Who knows. It could be. Might mean someone is keeping a close watch on everything here." He narrowed his eyes in thought. "Just because Oberon staked out a tiny bit of this world to hold Titania doesn't necessarily mean he knew anything about the remainder of it."

I took a step back, flummoxed by the implication. "Damn. Are you suggesting a *Spy-Versus-Spy* motif? Where the Unseelie were keeping an eye on Oberon? I doubt he visited frequently, but it would have been very like him to stop by and gloat."

"It's exactly what I'm suggesting. Think about it. The King of Winter planned to jettison Oberon once Faery was secure and he was no longer needed. What if Oberon had a secret strategy the king knew nothing about? Titania would have been quite the drawing card."

I frowned. "Not quite seeing that. It's not as if Oberon cared about her."

"Oh but he did," Cyn tossed out. "If he hadn't, he wouldn't have gone to all the trouble of making her comfortable. He'd have banished her to the *Dreaming* and made certain she couldn't leave."

"Ick." A shudder ran through me. "He didn't want her around, but didn't want anyone else to have her, either. That's just wrong. What kind of secret strategy?"

"He would have left himself an out, and my guess was it included Titania in some respect. More power was imbued in those doors that was necessary, a whole lot more."

Cyn directed a thin beam of power at the dappled area that hadn't felt quite like it belonged. This time, he probed, forcing his way past the surface. I'm not sure what I was expecting—in truth, I wasn't anticipating much of anything—but a muted boom rolled toward us.

Darkness fell like a chiaroscuro curtain. One moment we'd stood in sunlight. The next I needed to kindle a mage light to see anything. "Douse it," Cyn hissed.

The light had been instinctive. I killed it and switched to my third eye; a macabre psychic landscape spread around me. It was disturbing enough, I checked our warding one more time, needing it to be complete. It was. Where the daylight version of this place had been verdant, bucolic, this iteration was warped. Dried out dirt and boulders scattered every which way as if we'd stumbled into a giants' bowling alley. If the gentle hills I'd noticed in the distance were still there, I couldn't see them.

I felt Cyn working on a teleport spell. "We can't leave." I pitched my voice very low. "Not until we know more."

"Staying is a bad idea," he whispered back. "The birds must have been spies."

"You can't know that." Protectiveness surged. I'd liked them. Felt sorry for them and angry at whatever had frightened them.

He bent until his mouth was near my ear. "I don't need to lay eyes on the Unseelie. There's something about their power; I've begun catching whiffs of it. You weren't raised with them, so it wouldn't be obvious to you."

Jumping on a fast track to educate myself, I sorted threads of various magics comparing them with how the Unseelie had felt when they'd invaded Dubrova Castle. Not exactly a slam dunk, but close enough. How could I have missed something so obvious?

*Because I wasn't looking for it, and I should have been.*

Cyn nudged me. "This isn't working."

I snapped my focus back to him. He must mean teleporting out of here wasn't exactly coming together. Magic can be persnickety like that. Often when I've needed it most was when it turned into a fickle bitch and stuck its tongue out at me. I tracked the bones of his spell and couldn't fault it.

"Everything is where it should be." I latched onto his gaze. Worry had turned his burnished metal eyes more golden.

"Yeah. I've goosed it a couple of times, but more magic isn't our ticket out of here."

"Something has to be." I infused confidence into my words and shuffled through possibilities like a riverboat card shark.

"One would think." He gripped my hand, and we loped back in the direction we'd come. Assuming what we'd seen at first was pure illusion, it took a whole lot of magic to change the appearance of an entire environment.

"Which one is real?" I asked.

"Don't know, but probably this one. Titania never would have known."

I nodded, growing smarter by the moment. "Which would explain why her castle was underground. No day-night cues."

"Exactly. Ysir told us only a couple of the distant worlds were habitable. Maybe this one only meets that criteria with huge infusions of magic."

"But it looked normal when we showed up."

"That might have been part of the guards' task. To make it look ordinary on the rare occasions when mages dropped in. They weren't completely dead when we left with Titania."

I exhaled noisily. "Sure. And their magic wouldn't have fallen apart until all of them died."

The farther we ran, the worse the landscape looked. Bones and rotting corpses, human and animal, joined the unending vista of dried-out earth. Was there water here? Had the hawks been illusion too? Or shapeshifters working for the Unseelie. Where had the people and animals come from?

My next step plunged sideways unexpectedly. I pitched facedown, twisting an ankle on the edge of the hole leading to Titania's erstwhile dungeon. Cyn hauled me upright, but an idea gathered momentum.

"No coincidences," I muttered. "I've always been lucky, and someone was watching out for me. For us. Come on. I have an idea that might spring us from this joint." Moving gingerly until magic could heal my ankle, I lowered myself into the hole and splayed my hands over the runes on the doors.

"What are you thinking?" Cyn asked softly.

"Ssht. Let me work." The runes had kept Titania locked within. I'd neutralized that part of them, but they contained a tremendous amount of residual power. As first one and then another took on a soft glow, my confidence grew.

The sound of bare feet slapping against dirt was faint

at first, but growing closer fast. I pushed harder, harvesting the magic in the runes and adding it to Cyn's and mine.

"Kindle your spell," I ground out. "Do it now."

So much magic ran through me I expected to burst into a shower of sparks. I've been there before where I channeled too much. I'd pay for this, but an Unseelie army was bearing down on us. I could smell their magic now that I'd sorted it from everything else.

The subterranean cavern shattered. We floated in darkness courtesy of Cyn's teleport casting. I was huffing for air, heart pounding from the effort I'd expended.

"Nice work," Cynwrigg said.

"And not a moment too soon," I panted. "By all the gods, they nearly had us."

"Having and holding onto are two different things."

My mouth twisted into a wry grin. "Weren't you the one yammering on about optimism a little bit ago? We barely made it out of there. If my gambit hadn't worked, we'd be staring down the maw of an Unseelie horde."

"Almost doesn't count. It did work. Whatever possessed you to think about the doors?"

"You mentioned they held untapped possibilities a few moments ago, but I was who neutralized a few of those runes," I reminded him. "So I knew how much strength they had. Unraveling them was beyond Titania's ability, and she's quite formidable." I shook myself, working the kinks out of my neck and back. "All those birds and animals...?"

"The birds were probably shapeshifters. The animals like as not part of the illusion."

"But we slogged through dead ones." A shudder ran through me.

Breath whistled from between his teeth. "Can't explain that part. Why I couldn't sense the birds' magic bothers the crap out of me. One was touching me for god's sake. It should have been a surefire giveaway."

"The dead world was the real one, wasn't it?"

"My take," he said. "Hold on. We're nearly back."

"That was fast."

"We're running on rune power. The question of the day is how we'll field an army big enough to take them on. If a critical mass of dragons are willing to help, we might prevail."

"We could throw ourselves on the gods' goodwill. Or their pity." I reminded him of our earlier conversation.

"We won't leave any stones unturned. That's a given."

The stairs below Lady Luck came into view. Good. Walking the last bit into Faery would settle my nerves. Close calls are one thing, suicide missions quite another. "I've probably watched too many *Star Trek* episodes, but is there some way we can simply blow up that whole world?" I asked.

"Maybe. It's an excellent idea. Even that would

COURT OF THE FALLEN

require a strike team to plant explosives. They'd be powered by magic, but we'd still have to get them there." He looped an arm around me and drew me close. "How's your foot?"

"Almost healed." I allowed myself a small luxury and wrapped my arms behind his back, holding on tight.

"You're shaking."

"Adrenaline overload is a bitch." I tried for humor, but probably came up short.

"Do you want to turn around?"

"And go where?" I did not want to go back to the place we'd escaped from by the skin of our teeth. I'd be damned if I'd admit it, though. Not much rattles me, but the narrow margin that had spelled the difference between victory and annihilation turned my bones to icy shards.

"To Earth. Either the casino or your flat. We could catch a meal, rest up a bit. Once we cross Faery's borders, we'll be in the thick of strategizing until we have a viable plan to wipe out the Unseelie and their perverse world."

It felt like cheating, like playing hooky when the school needed my presence, or it would collapse. "Are you certain we can afford the time?"

He tilted my chin until his gaze bored into me. "We can't not afford it. Are you running on all cylinders? I'm sucking fumes. The next phase will require us to be at the top of our game. I'm not, and neither are you."

I winced. His assessment was accurate, but it still rankled. Appearing weak isn't part of my character, but I felt like a used-up dishrag courtesy of all the power that had run through me.

"Sold." I aimed for jaunty, but missed it by a mile.

"Smart woman. Where do you want to go?"

"My flat? We can get takeout from the Chinese place at the end of the block."

"Excellent. Your chariot has arrived."

I sank into his spell. He may have done something because I was almost asleep when the walls of my empty flat came into view. I remember Midnight streaking to me before I curled up in a ball on the carpet and passed out.

# CHAPTER FOUR, CYN

I curved my body around Dariyah and the cat after I'd checked the empty apartment for threats. For all my bravado, we'd had an exceedingly close call. If I'd been by myself, I'd still be stuck on the remote world hiding and plotting my egress. Maybe. If I'd been fortunate, concealing myself would have worked. Except the birds had sensed our presence.

Perhaps they'd been reacting to Dariyah's unusual blend of magics, or perhaps something about that world turned normal spells into hash. I watched the gentle rise and fall of Dariyah's chest. She looked tired, with dark smudges under her eyes and creases in her forehead that sleep hadn't quite erased.

I'd have done almost anything to spare her what lay in our immediate future, yet she was an instrumental part of it. She had to be. Auril had groomed her for what was shaping up to be a major showdown with her father. I'd lay money on Auril holding back information even now. She'd never been the forthcoming type on the best of days, and she'd turned subterfuge into an art form. She must have had absolute faith in whatever visions had first led her to the winged horse and then pushed her to hide her child from the world until she'd come into her full power.

Rehashing history was usually a waste of time, but I kept hoping I'd glean some critical tidbits I'd missed. Items that might clarify which moves would return Faery to us.

Left to my own devices, I'd never have thought to harness the residual magic in the runes. More accurately, even if I'd considered them, I lacked the skill to harvest that source of additional magic.

It suggested Pegasus—or one of the Gorgons—had something to do with imprisoning Titania. The spell that held her captive was cunningly woven, using her magic to ensure she'd never be able to find a way out. When she summoned power, the enchantment holding her grew stronger too.

It was a lose-lose proposition. For her. And well beyond Oberon's command of spellcraft, but I bet he held the keys to unravel it. If he'd requested assistance as I suspected, the ability to take the spell apart had probably been one of his requirements. What in the hell had he traded for such an elaborate undertaking? His assistance handing over Faery had probably been part of the package. I'd have given a lot to know everything, but some secrets are destined to remain hidden.

I'd had my head propped onto an upraised hand. Taking care not to disturb Dariyah, I got up and looked through a couple of closets and cupboards until I found the bedding she'd brought from her other apartment. After tucking a quilt around her legs and a pillow beneath her head, I lay back down, resting my head on the second pillow.

I don't require much in the way of sleep, but closing my eyes was welcome. It didn't slow my thoughts, but at least the imagery from that stark world faded a notch or two. The cat was purring like a miniature steam engine, the sound homey and soothing. After a time, I stopped trying to tack down every detail about what came next.

I'd convene the court, along with Auril and Ysir, and we'd brainstorm our next steps. It hadn't been Oberon's style. He made decisions, plopped them in front of everyone, and expected compliance. Of course, he also played a masterful blame game when his edicts turned to shit. Failures were never his fault. Oh hell, no. They fell squarely on the shoulders of his minions who'd failed to read between the lines of his orders and anticipate unexpected outcomes.

Thank all the gods I wasn't him. Although I'm far from fond of Earth and mortals, they do a few things rather well some of the time. One of those includes paying lip service to democratic process. Many minds are always better than one, and everyone has something solid to contribute.

Dariyah turned in her sleep, burrowed deeper into the pillow, and tossed an arm over me. I gathered her close, careful not to disturb her. Midnight wasn't pleased with the new arrangement. After a muted yowl of discontent, he clawed his way from between our bodies and settled in the hollow between Dariyah's neck and shoulder.

My feverish mental maneuverings weren't buying me much, so I shut everything down and dozed fitfully. I didn't want to sink too deep in case someone found us. The odds were thin. Dariyah had warded her new flat, but then she'd done the same with the old one. It hadn't slowed Oberon down much.

More awake than asleep again, I considered the mismatch between Oberon's magic and Dariyah's. He hadn't been able to penetrate her Witch glamour, which suggested he'd had help locating her once she'd confronted him about being a skinflint.

The reason our paths had crossed—although they may have been destined to do so anyway—was because he'd hired her to spy on me, a task she'd gladly taken on. Until the day some of his henchmen told her the job was over and she had to accept half wages or nothing.

Oberon hadn't counted on Dariyah's temper. Or the fact money wasn't much of a motivator for her. She'd thrown down a gauntlet, challenged him, and things had become interesting. He'd sent several groups of mages to do away with her. When that failed, he'd targeted Midnight.

The same anger that festered whenever I thought about the tom-cat suffering at Oberon's hands flared. How dare he?

"You're thinking so loud, I can't sleep," Dariyah murmured near my ear.

"Sorry. I'll tone it down." I cradled the back of her head with one hand and kneaded tense muscles.

"It's all right. I never sleep much, and I've probably had enough." She threw a leg over my thigh and molded her body to mine. "Did you solve all our problems? Or did you at least manage to get some rest?"

"Aye to the latter. Nay to the former. We need both the court and Faery's citizens to voice their opinions. Whatever we do next holds significant risks for everyone."

"What happens if we lose Faery?"

I didn't have an answer for her, so I said, "I don't know. We'd be in totally uncharted waters."

"Have the Unseelie had a home since they left Faery?"

Mmph. Didn't have the answer for that one, either. "My guess is we were just there."

"Jesus. No wonder they're in such a horrid mood. What a grim place to live."

I drew back enough to look at her. Her lips were tempting, full, and parted with just the tip of her tongue visible. Because I couldn't help myself, couldn't resist, I lowered my mouth to hers and kissed her. I'd only meant for our lips to touch as a sign of caring, but the moment our mouths connected, heat and need and desperation rose from my belly.

She turned to quicksilver in my arms, molten and flowing. Every place she touched me ignited, and our scents eddied about us thickened by undernotes of pure musk. The peaks of her breasts sent shock waves through my chest. Where she'd tossed a leg over my thigh, heat from her rolled through me in waves. My cock, which had already begun to thicken, turned rock-hard.

Every iteration of being has celebrated narrow escapes with sex, almost as if it wiped the slate clean and offered a new beginning. I rolled her onto her back and sat on top of her while I tugged her blouse up to bare her breasts. Breath caught in my throat at the sight of them. Twin creamy globes tipped with copper nipples the size of silver dollars, they sat high and proud on her chest.

I filled my hands with them, rubbing and rolling the already distended nipples. She kicked her head back, neck corded with passion and blotched with strawberry patches that spread downward until they dappled her breasts too.

Bending my head, I took a nipple in my mouth, lashing my tongue back and forth. Magnificent mewling purrs bubbled from her throat, and her hands busied themselves undoing my trousers. I hadn't planned to make love to her, but it would have taken a tsunami rolling through her living room to stop us now.

I'd switched to the other nipple and then back again to the first as my fingertips explored the hot silk of skin stretched taut over her ribcage. A hand closed around my achingly hard erection. The skin-to-skin contact nearly blew the top of my head off, and I draped magic around my arousal to keep it contained.

She drummed her fingers up and down the length of my shaft, swirled them around the head, and continued variations of the same. My breath was coming in shallow pants. Every cell in my body was primed to claim her and make her mine.

Forever.

The revelation was startling. I'd read about such things, but never believed in them. Letting go of her nipple was excruciating. I straightened and closed a hand over the one busy stroking my cock. "This will be permanent," I croaked, my voice thick with passion.

Her eyes fluttered open. "Permanent?"

"Aye. Like a mating ceremony but without the vows or binding magic."

"How can you know?" She pushed to a sit and let go of me long enough to pull her top over her head. I scooted back until I knelt near her feet. While she was at it, she removed my shirt too. I was so aroused, just the air currents in the room touching my nipples were erotic as hell.

I took her hand. "I don't. Not for certain, but I wanted to make certain you understood this might bind us in...well, in ways you might not be prepared for."

"Are you?" Her green-eyed gaze was sheened with lust.

"Aye. Having you by my side forever would be a dream, an honor."

She smiled, slow and lazy. It started in her eyes and moved to her mouth. "Me too. Let's get rid of these clothes." She kicked the quilt aside. "Oh! When did you take my boots off?"

"When I got the quilt." Sliding my hands down her naked torso did odd things to my mind. She was perfect, so flawless I longed to eat her up with my eyes—and every other part of me. I unfastened her pants and tugged them down her long legs as I strung kisses down her belly.

She'd jackknifed her body around and pulled my trousers out of the way. No boots on my feet, either. So long as I was removing hers, I'd taken mine off too. At the time, I'd wondered how smart it was in case something happened and we had to move quickly, but I'd opted for comfort.

"Christ on a crutch, but you're lovely." She trailed her hands down my body. Not that I needed more stimulation, but her touch on my skin made me long to spirit her away to a place where there would only be us. Where we could make love in ten thousand inventive ways, resurface, and come up with ten thousand more.

Wherever she stroked me, my soul caught fire. I maneuvered around until I knelt over her once again. She wrapped her legs around my waist and guided my cock until it rested against the opening to her body. Placing a hand over hers, I moved in small circles, teasing her hot, slick places. She arched her back, bucking against me, but I held back.

Once I was inside her, the fire licking at our heels would engulf us. I wanted this to last. Sweet, delicious urgency enveloped us as our magic slammed together. Having developed a will of its own, it propelled us forward.

She let go of my cock and gripped my hips with both

hands, her intent clear as the mirrors her mother used to scry the future. I slipped inside. Just an inch or so, the sensation so intense it wiped everything from my mind.

A ragged gasp from her, and vibration from our conjoined magics, told me she was as blown away as me. Dariyah dug her nails into my hips urging me forward. "More, goddammit," she growled. "Whole lot of unused real estate."

I'd been teasing her nipples and moved a hand to her distended clit, rubbing in small circles. Her hips bucked. "Harder. Do it harder," she moaned.

Joined with her mind and her magic, I followed her climax as it began deep within her, altering the rhythm of my fingers to push her as high as she could go. When the wave crested and washed over both of us, it was all I could do not to join her. The head of my cock tingled, burning with need. Still, I waited until her climax played itself out before I pushed the rest of the way inside.

Slowly. Ever so slowly, despite a driving need to plunge into her at the speed of light. She writhed beneath me, groaning and panting and hanging onto my ass as I withdrew equally slowly. My own climax could wait until she was on the verge of another.

I could do this.

She tightened around me, vault fluttering with lust. My next strokes weren't quite as measured. Breath burned in my throat, reminding me breathing was a good idea. The air around us developed jewel tones as our magic formed colored streamers that twisted around us. Everywhere they touched made me hotter, higher.

What control I'd managed exploded as I drove into her with a fury unmatched in my long life. Love crashed through me, mixed with lust and desire as sharp as raw diamonds. She met me stroke for stroke, and we strained against one another.

"Yes," she cried. "Now."

My body wasn't my own any longer. It answered to her. My balls had been snugged against my crotch since her first peak. Jism flowed upward and turned into an orgasm that went on forever. At some point, I'd bent forward and crushed my mouth over hers. Our teeth and tongues tangled as passion roared through us.

We ended up in a heap, gasping and panting and pushing against one another. Eventually, the pressure to be as close as we could be lessened. While far from gone, it had lost its desperate edges.

"Mmmm. Delicious," she purred and nipped my lip.

"At least you have words. They fail me."

She tugged a long strand of her hair from between our bodies. "Is that good or bad?"

"Someplace beyond good."

She smiled. "Wow! High praise, but we should get back to Faery."

"Aye, but the extra half hour we stole for ourselves won't make any difference."

Dariyah snuggled close. "Or all the difference in all the worlds. I felt something shift, change while our magics were doing that lovely dance all around us."

Her eyes were warm, soft, liquid with the passion we'd shared. She was waiting for me to agree. "Not sure about a change. I was so immersed in you, there wasn't anything else in my heart or my mind."

"Yeah. That too, but"—she tapped her breastbone —"something altered. In here. My magic has new elements."

I'd been rubbing her neck and shoulders beneath her thick fall of hair. I moved down, massaging the cords of muscles stretching over bone. Bumps perched over her shoulder blades. They radiated magic as I explored them. "Did you ever have wings?"

She laughed. "Nope. Wing buds, but they fell off. I figured they were courtesy of my Sidhe half, until I discovered I don't have a Sidhe half. Where you're touching me is where they were, but I'm surprised you can feel anything. They've been gone for centuries."

Because I'd been stroking them, I felt them growing. "Sweetling, maybe you should take a look in the mirror. I don't know how they looked before."

"Do I have to let go of you?"

"Not really. Only if you want to." Tiny feathers were

sprouting, covering the rapidly growing bumps. I kissed her forehead and her cheeks and helped her to her feet. We padded to the bathroom where she angled herself between two mirrors and moved the fall of her hair aside.

"Gawk. They never looked like that. Ever." Angling a hand backward, she tried to touch one of what were shaping up to be tiny wings but couldn't quite reach it. Our eyes met in the mirror in front of us. The softness had fled from hers, replaced by worry. "Do you know what's happening to me?"

I could hazard a guess, but how close it would be to accurate remained to be seen. For that, we'd need Auril or Ysir with their seer talents.

"Cyn?"

Mounting panic in her voice smote me; I gathered her into my arms. "My guess, and it's only a guess, is something about us making love kicked open a gate for you to fully claim your magic. Auril may have done something to block Pegasus's half of your heritage, but you sealing a bond with your one true mate defeated her casting."

"I'm going to have wings?" Dariyah shook her head. "Not sure I like that. They'll be clumsy. None of my clothes will fit. Eh." She rolled her eyes. "Talk about inconsequential crap."

I still held her close. The baby wings were at least

two inches longer. Covered by soft silvery feathers, they'd be breathtaking once they finished coming in. "They won't be clumsy once you learn to use them," I said. "Think about it. You'll be able to fly. I think I'm jealous."

Midnight streaked into the bathroom and jumped onto the ledge. Dariyah stroked his head. Our lovemaking may have chased him off, but he seemed oblivious to her wings.

"Let's find you something to wear," I said. "Once we're back in Faery, you can ask your mother about my theory."

"I bet she already knows. One more thing to add to the list of what she neglected to tell me," Dariyah mumbled and untangled herself from my embrace. "Here I was feeling delighted by stronger magic. Guess everything has a price."

I dropped a hand onto her shoulder. "I love you. You. Wings don't matter. I fell in love with you without them, and I'll still love you with them."

She closed her teeth over her lower lip. "Thanks. There's so much right now. The last thing I need is new body parts to learn about."

"The dragons can give you a crash course in flight." I snapped my fingers. "That's it."

"What's it?" We walked back to where we'd left our

discarded clothing. She pulled on her pants and boots and sat looking at her top.

"We'll start at Fire Mountain. They have their own seers. You can work on flying, and then we'll return to Faery." I dragged garments on as I spoke.

"But my wings won't be big enough."

"Oh yeah, they will. They've added six inches since we left the bathroom. And Dariyah."

"Yes?"

"They're beautiful, and so are you. Do you have maybe a bra top and a cloak you could toss over everything?"

It took some experimenting, but we located a low-backed stretchy top that accommodated her growing wings. She snapped her Witch glamour into place, and they disappeared from view. Meant she could still pass as mortal here on Earth.

"Ready to leave?" she asked and bent to stroke Midnight's soft, black fur. He batted at a wing with his paws, meowing approvingly.

"Earlier you'd mentioned food. Are you hungry? Do we need to grab something to take with us?"

Dariyah shook her head. "Between the amazing sex and these"—she flipped a wing—"eating isn't in the cards. Maybe later, but not right now."

I summoned a teleport spell and draped it around us both. Sometimes fewer words are better. I'd said all I needed to about the wings, but she had to come to terms with them. We both understood they weren't just wings but a physical reminder of who'd fathered her, something she was a long way from accepting.

Dariyah ginned up a wan smile. "Thanks for being such a rock."

I smiled back. "That's me. Granite could be my middle name. We'll get through this."

"Damn. I sure as fuck hope so."

"Hope not, just do."

She laughed. "Thanks Yoda."

I kindled my spell, and her living room dropped away. The dragons would shed light—maybe more than we wanted—on Dariyah's transition. I'd meant what I said, though. I'd always wanted wings, but having a mate with them was the next best thing. Before I got lost in wondering whether our children—if we had any—would carry that particular gene, I opened my magic to Dariyah's to speed our journey.

"Take all you want," she said. "Seems like I have power to burn."

"Don't kick a gift horse in the mouth."

"I'm not." She threaded her fingers with mine. "Everything has a price. If wings are the price of whatever my newly enhanced magic brings us, they might be worth it."

"They will be. You gotta believe."

"First tenet of magic," she teased back.

"You know it is. Get ready. Fire Mountain is closer than it used to be."

"I am curious what those seers of theirs will have to say."

I squeezed her hand. She was moving past shock to curiosity. Good thing, since her wings reached her waist and looked as if they were nearly formed. With little fanfare, my casting shattered around us, and we tumbled through the hot, dry air of Fire Mountain. Or rather, I fell. Dariyah instinctively spread her wings and floated to the ground, while I scrabbled to cobble enough magic together to break my descent.

## CHAPTER FIVE, DARIYAH

So much for the cloak I'd arranged over my wings. It fell off the moment I spread them to break my fall. Not that I thought about any of it. There wasn't time. Like an automatic, built-in parachute, the wings deployed, creating airfoils. It was eerie and amazing rolled into one. After a couple of experimental flaps that didn't feel nearly as clumsy as I'd feared, I drifted onto the burning sand.

Nothing about this place had changed. Why should it? The twin suns sat slightly past midheaven, and the hot dry air scoured my mouth and throat. I tucked an arm over the lower part of my face to breathe through and fanned my wings to move the air around.

Cyn had said he loved me. I hadn't quite absorbed that, either. It would have been an opportunity to tell him how I felt, but I'd held back. A lifetime of hiding my feelings wouldn't dissipate overnight, but he'd become the center of my universe not long after I'd hired on as Oberon's right-hand gal to shadow him. During those months, I'd skirted away from the truth, even convinced myself I could walk away, but I'd been full of it.

The only way Cynwrigg could have gotten rid of me was by telling me to get lost, and not even that would have worked very well. My pride would have been hurt. I'd have made a show of leaving, but whether I could have stayed gone or not was uncertain.

I'd never given more than a passing thought to mates or marriage or permanency. Living my life from the shadows didn't lend itself to anything lasting—like a man. Or even friends if you put a finer point on it. Mother had done a bang-up job preparing me to flee at a moment's notice. I didn't even have to be certain someone was onto me. If I waited to check things out, it might be too late.

Nope. At the first sign I might have been compromised, I was to run. I'd jettisoned many of Mother's tenets, but not that one. My survival depended on remaining alert. I understood full well I was taking a chance working for Oberon, and I'd been poised to flee until it grew clear he had no idea who I was and didn't appear likely to figure it out.

Maybe Titania had been onto something when she'd said I'd been drawn to Oberon because of my Fae blood. That I couldn't have avoided him if I'd tried. I didn't believe her at the time, and I still don't. But then, I'd been the one who'd snatched that posting off the job board at the mage-for-hire place. It hadn't exactly had Oberon's name plastered all over it, but something about the ad snagged my attention.

So much so, I'd tapped the relevant information into my phone and emailed right away. We all like to believe we're free agents. It makes us believe we're independent, but in this case, I'd waltzed right into a velvet-lined trap that had my future stenciled into it.

Thank all the gods for my ironclad glamour. Anything less, and my goose would have been cooked. Or maybe everything that had happened was foreordained somehow and free will nothing but illusion. I'd clearly been meant to meet Cynwrigg, and it never would have happened if I hadn't answered the posting on that job board.

"See. Told you those wings would come in handy." Cyn somersaulted to the ground next to me. "When you spread them, it looked instinctive, not awkward at all."

I elbowed him. "No one likes a know-it-all."

"That was a compliment."

A snort bubbled out. "I've gotten so few I'm not that great at recognizing them. Appears we've been discovered." I angled my gaze skyward at three dragons winging their way to where we stood. Rocking from foot to foot eased the burn from the hot earth beneath my boot soles.

I tried to swallow, but the superheated air had sucked every iota of moisture from my mouth. What would the dragons do? No hiding my wings. As they drew nearer, I recognized the two blind seers. The larger golden dragon with them might have been the same one who'd accompanied them to Faery.

They skidded in for a landing, tossing hot sand every which way. The seers turned their milk white eyes my way and closed from both sides exchanging comments in their language. Unfortunately, I couldn't understand them—and I wanted to.

"English, please," I said. "Or Gaelic or any modern language except maybe Chinese."

Cyn stood so near our sides touched. He bowed his head briefly and said, "Many thanks for your hospitality."

The larger dragon hooted laughter. Smoke and flames accompanied it. "If that's a backhanded way of reminding us to invite you inside, you're correct it wasn't at the forefront of my mind."

A seer had moved behind me and touched one of my wings. It felt strange, and would have been even stranger if Cyn hadn't spent time stroking them when they were growing in. Sweat cascaded down my body. I swiped a forearm across my face to keep it from dripping into my eyes.

"Follow us, if you will," the other seer said and did an about face. As I trudged after him, I felt lightheaded from the pounding glare of the sun. Magic can protect me from a whole lot of things, but heat isn't one of them. Hot spots on my feet turned to blisters, and I was grateful my ankle had managed to put itself back together.

Cyn had hold of my hand. Where our palms had been sweaty at first, now they were so dry it was painful where they rubbed together. How much farther could the cave where we'd sheltered before possibly be?

"Soon," Cyn said softly, proving he'd been inside my mind. Maybe that part of our binding was permanent, but I was too woozy to test my end of the connection. My head spun, and I tripped over a rock I should have been able to avoid. When my wings shot out for balance, one wrapped around Cyn.

"I will never get used to them," I croaked.

"Of course you will." The seer walking behind us sounded far too cheerful for my liking.

A cliff reared up out of nowhere, and the glare of the sun winked out as we entered the dragons' underground lair. I was panting, gasping for air that didn't bake my insides. The large dragon led the way to the same rushing creek where I'd slaked my thirst my first visit here.

"May we partake of your water?" Cyn asked.

I was grateful to him because my voice was as trashed as the rest of me.

"Please," the dragon said. "Once you are refreshed, you will accompany us to our council chamber. We have convened a special session."

I didn't especially like the sound of that, but I tottered forward and fell on my knees next to the creek. The wings added ballast I wasn't used to, but I forgot all about them as I cupped cool water in my hands and rinsed them and my face before slugging back as much as I could drink.

When I looked up, the walls of the cavern had taken on an iridescent glow. Had it been here before? I couldn't recall. Cyn rocked back on his heels and swiped away water running down his chin. "Did you have enough?"

Nodding, I got to my feet. No one said anything as we filed out of the cavern and wound lower into the bowels of the cave system. While I was grateful for the relative coolness, the fine hairs on the back of my neck prickled with anxiety. I've never had even a whisper of seer talent, which is interesting given my mother's ability, but I felt certain whatever transpired over the next hour would change the shape of my life forever.

Would Cyn still be part of it?

He'd said he believed we were forever mates, but what if his role had been to activate my latent power?

"We are in this together," he said firmly.

"Aw geez. I'm sorry," I muttered. "My mind is too busy."

"Mine too. Seeing your true form verified something for the seers."

I cast a sidelong glance his way. Banks of tiny lights were recessed into the passageway walls, providing dim but usable illumination. "You understand their language?"

"I do."

My glance shaded to a glare. If Cyn had been inclined to tell me, he'd have done so.

"This way." The large dragon turned hard right into an opening I'd have walked right past. An enormous cavern lay before us with rows and rows of elevated seating that reminded me of an outdoor amphitheater. Except we were deep underground. The roundish chamber must have been two hundred feet in every direction, and the ceiling was so far above me I couldn't see it. The same recessed lights dotted the walls.

Dragons were everywhere. Reds, blues, greens, golds, blacks, and the occasional white beast. Mostly they stood, but some had settled onto the raised rows of benches. They were beautiful and intimidating. The smallest of them were the blind seers, and even they towered over me. Whatever they'd gleaned from seeing my wings hadn't scared Cyn off, but he wasn't the type to spook easily. He'd made a commitment to me—to us— that wasn't going anywhere.

I focused on that because all the rest of it was overwhelming. At least walking was beginning to feel normal. At first, the wings had been a counterweight requiring constant attention.

Cyn stood a few feet inside the arched doorway still holding onto my hand. No one offered us seats or appeared to have any preference for where we settled. Would it be disrespectful to sit?

Our host dragon bugled, and the rest of the flight faced the front of the room. While they were finding seats, the large golden dragon lumbered down an aisle to a dais at the bottom. Fire flared from his mouth, lighting a rush torch. It burned in many colors, and he set it into a holder off to one side.

"The dragons' council is in session," he boomed in Gaelic. It surprised me. I figured they'd chatter away in their own tongue, and I'd have to rely on Cyn to interpret for me.

The blind seers marched down the same aisle and took up positions on either side of the lead dragon. I assumed he was their leader. In truth, I had no idea how they were organized.

"Come forward," the nearest seer called. They looked so much alike, I decided I needed some way to differentiate them. The one who'd just spoken had wings a slightly paler shade of gold. He'd be Seer One.

I didn't realize "come forward" was meant for me until Cyn gave me a small shove. "It will be all right," he said softly.

I hastened down the walkway until I reached Seer One, keeping my gaze glued on him. Normally, I'm quick with the repartee, but this wasn't a venue for my smart mouth. My wings rustled as I walked. Geez. Were they still growing?

"Do not be afraid," the seer who'd summoned me said.

My usual bravado took a hike. "Hard not to be," I replied, matching his Gaelic. Once, long ago, it had been my primary language.

"We will tell you a story," Seer One went on.

"Aye," the other—Seer Two—chimed in. "'Tis a legend we first scryed eons ago, so long ago I'd nearly decided 'twas a false prophecy. Yet here you are."

I started to parrot "here I am," but decided against it. My role was to listen, to absorb, and to do my part once I understood what it entailed.

"We knew Auril coaxed Pegasus's seed from him," Seer One said. "It was the initial step in the legend we foresaw."

"Understanding you were that get, we were confused when we first met you," Seer Two said.

I ditched my commitment to silence and asked, "Why?"

"We saw your mother's lines in you, but naught of the winged horse," he replied.

"We discussed if our foreseeing could have stumbled," Seer One said.

"Such has never been the case before, but there is a first time for everything," Seer Two added.

"But we are getting ahead of ourselves. We must start at the beginning." Seer One spoke firmly. His words took on the singsong cadence I associated with bards from a time long past.

"Worlds come and go. Some are more robust than others, but nothing abides forever," he began. "Dragons are oldest of the Elderkin, and Fire Mountain one of the very first worlds, but even it has changed."

"When our world spun out of fire and the void"— Seer Two took up the tale—"there was no Faery. Magic was rare, special, and the purview of dragons. Everyone else was an afterthought."

Somehow, I didn't think the gods would interpret events in quite the same light, but I kept it to myself.

"When Faery formed from crystals and motes of light, she was a tall, striking woman in charge of a brand-new world," Seer Two continued. "Power blazed from her so brightly, we believed it in our best interest to join forces."

"You can skip over that part," the dragon in charge rumbled.

"But they might not know about it," the seer protested.

"Aye, everything is interconnected," Seer One tossed out. "We will shorten things up, though. After a promising beginning, Faery weakened. Part of it was Oberon's incessant greed and narrow-mindedness. We hoped when he departed things would improve. They didn't."

"You shortened up and rolled right over that one's"— Seer Two waved his talons in my direction—"conception and birth. During Faery's less-than-stellar decline, Auril made a few wise decisions. The first was walking away from the Unseelie lord she was mated to."

"Nay, the first was deciding not to have children with him," Seer One spoke up.

"That too," Seer Two agreed. "The blood of the gods runs strong in Auril. She and Titania share a father, but Danu was her mother."

My eyes widened. News to me. I'd asked about my grandparents and always gotten a royal runaround. Now I knew why. Danu was my grandmother. Did she know about me?

"I suspected you weren't aware of your lineage," Seer

Two went on. "In any event, Auril scryed an extraordinary vision, one so remarkable she made a trip to speak with us about it. We cast our own future-seeking spells and corroborated her version of what was to come. After that, she disguised herself as a mortal and sought out Pegasus in his human glamour."

My stomach twisted sourly. So far, I hadn't heard anything new, but that was about to change. I longed for Cyn next to me, but he hadn't been called forward. Only me.

I rolled my shoulders back, standing as tall as I could. Compared with the dragons, I was still a dwarf, but I'd face whatever this was head-on, like I dealt with everything. Running from unpleasantness has never been my style. I'd rather plow through obstacles and put them behind me.

*Lots of luck with that.* My caustic inner voice was back. She knew whatever this was would color my life for the foreseeable future. No putting anything behind me. Not this time.

"Auril knew full well she would have to hide you away." Seer One began talking again. "She forsook Faery willingly, even though it meant leaving everything and everyone she'd ever cared for."

"Because she understood she played a high-stakes game," Seer Two said. "The highest stakes ever. Faery's very existence was at risk. If she'd done nothing, not lain with Pegasus, Faery was doomed to fade into oblivion. Auril's altruism provided a champion to wrest Faery back from the ragged edge of destruction."

"The land will never look the same, but at least it has a chance of continuing." Seer One nodded knowingly.

"It would have been nice if she'd have told me," I mumbled.

"How could she have?" Seer Two questioned. "Any knowledge you held could be stolen from you. If your enemies, who presumably had access to the same prophecy, discovered who you were, they'd have made certain you never lived to fulfill your part of it."

Invitation be damned, Cynwrigg had joined me. "What role do I play?"

"You unlocked her full power," Seer Two replied.

"Aye, you are her mate. We shall seal your troth with blood and fire so it's unbreakable," Seer One chimed in.

"Did Mother know that part?" I demanded.

"Not precisely," the seer answered. "We understood a key existed, yet none of us knew what it was. It remained hidden for the same reason you did. If the Unseelie or the Gorgons had recognized Cynwrigg's role, he'd never have made it past childhood, much less ended up regent of Faery."

"Who is behind all this?" Cyn asked.

The seers shrugged in unison. "We assume the dark gods, particularly given Danu's connection to Auril, but we are not certain," Seer One replied. "There has always been great antipathy between the fallen gods and those who pay homage to Danu."

"Pulling things together," the dragon's leader broke in, "we have a prophecy that states Faery will diminish until she no longer exists unless drastic measures are taken. She"—he pointed a long, red talon dead center at my chest—"will be Faery's champion."

"Not going to go over very well," I muttered. "She hates me."

"Once she reclaims her body, your standing will improve," the immense golden dragon retorted.

"She has to want to recover her physical essence," Cynwrigg said. "When I suggested it, she appeared lukewarm."

"Not our problem," the dragon said. "Our role is working with that one." He pointed at me again.

It pissed me off. "Look. I have a name."

"Aye, you do, and 'tisn't Dariyah, but it will do for now."

"What are yours?" I was sick of labeling the seers as one and two and the other one as leader.

"We are Goren and Brynn," one of the seers said, adding, "I am Goren."

"We will oversee your training," Brynn said.

"How long will we be here?" Cyn asked.

"No need for you to remain," the lead dragon, who

still hadn't offered his name, said. The more I thought about it, the surer I was he had to be Ash, the dragon who'd been my escort last time.

"What if I want him to?" I asked.

"Faery needs him," the dragon retorted. "We require your undivided attention. Two or three days should do it now that your magic has been unlocked."

"I will make good use of the time." Cynwrigg bowed formally. "What have you seen about the war? Should we include the gods? Will you fight beside us? Dariyah and I located the Unseelie's staging area. We'd thought to begin there to limit their numbers."

"Come with us." The seers tried to herd me up the aisle.

I gave Cyn a quick hug. "I'll return as quickly as I can."

He held me tight before letting go. As I followed the seers, I heard the dragons' leader say, "Definitely include the gods, and of course we will fly for your cause. 'Tis ours as well. If Faery fails, Fire Mountain won't be far behind."

We'd reached the central corridor carved into the heart of Fire Mountain. "Is he your king or your prince?" I asked.

"Neither. He is the embodiment of Fire Mountain. Much like Faery would be if she still had her body," Brynn told me.

I took a chance. "He is called Ash, right?"

"It is but one of his many names," Goren replied.

The seers turned right, and we continued downhill. "Where are we going?"

"To our practice arena. We have another above ground, but we will be at this for a while. We do not believe training above ground would suit you."

Goren's words held a formal note, but I could have kissed him. "Thank you."

"Nay, it is us who should be thanking you. The fate of magical worlds rests on your shoulders. 'Tis a heavy weight, and not a welcome one." They stopped walking and turned to face me. "Think long and hard," he went on. "Do you accept this burden and all it entails?"

"If you harbor the slightest doubts," Brynn said, "now is the time to voice them. Once we cross the next barrier, your fate is sealed, and there will be no way out except through."

A spark of anger licked at me. Damn Mother. She'd known and said nothing. I might understand her reasoning, but it would take some doing before I forgave her. And then I kicked myself roundly. She was only doing what she had to. She'd walked away from her life for a higher purpose. How could I possibly offer less?

"Only a fool has no doubts," I said, "but I will pick up the banner and do my best."

Goren chanted a few words, and we walked into a

well-lighted enclosure. "Your first lessons," he said and offered a toothy grin, "will revolve around using your wings. Something dragons excel at."

"Aye, you couldn't wish for better teachers." Brynn leapt skyward.

After a moment's hesitation, I joined him. My initial shock about the wings was receding. Flight was a gift. A joy. And a hell of a lot easier to wrap my mind around than being some sort of sacrificial sheep leading Faery to either victory or her doom.

## ❧ 6 ❧

## CHAPTER SIX, CYN

My thoughts were a blur as I left Fire Mountain. I was so lost in mapping out strategies I barely noticed the wall of heat as I left the caves. Ash, Fire Mountain's eternal leader, had offered me an escort, but I'd declined. It was enough he'd committed wings, scales, and talons to our battle. I didn't require a nursemaid on my trip back to Faery.

What I wasn't certain of was what to tell Titania and Auril about Dariyah. Turned out it was a non-issue. I'd no sooner emerged near the Midnight Court when Auril hurried to me.

It was full dark, so I didn't see her spring forward, but she latched onto my arm with a death grip. When she kindled a mage light, it burned so bright I shielded my eyes.

"It is done," she hissed. "Don't bother denying it."

I shook free with difficulty. "Dariyah and I sealed our commitment to one another, if that is your question."

Auril canted her light at a different angle so it wasn't shining right into my eyes. "She claimed the other half of her parentage. It was what I foresaw. The part that eluded me was the precise mechanism." The queen of air and darkness shook her head until red tresses bounced around her shoulders. "Stupid of me. I should have known it would be you."

"How could you have?" I countered.

Forming a circle with her hands, she said, "Events unfold for reasons of their own. In this instance, my daughter crossed paths with Oberon for the express purpose of meeting you. If magic weren't in play, she'd never have engaged in something so perilous."

I wasn't certain about that. Dariyah was a far different woman than the one who'd left Auril's side years and years before. "Do you know who's orchestrating this?" I asked her the same question I'd asked Ash.

"On which side?" Her mouth twisted into a sour expression.

"Either one. The more I understand, the better prepared we'll be."

"Did you find them?" Ysir rushed forward.

"If by them, you mean the Unseelie, aye. They're on

the same world where Titania was held prisoner, but it's a grim place. Nothing like it appeared when we freed her from bondage."

He nodded sharply. "Like I told you, only two of the distant worlds are habitable. Someone employed illusion to alter that one. I have troops ready to deploy. When do we leave?"

"Whoa. No troops until we have a whole lot more tacked down." My tone held a warning note on purpose. The last thing we needed was to race off half-cocked, sending a chunk of our forces the equivalent of light years away. For all I knew, the King of Winter had posted spies who'd alert him to just such a development.

"What more do we require?" Ysir focused his shrewd gaze my way.

"A coordinated plan. The dragons said they'd help, but I'm leaning toward a remote approach where we blow that whole world to bits, scattering it and its inhabitants."

"Someone would still need to travel there to plant magic-laced explosives," Ysir said.

"Which also requires careful thought and planning." I blew out a tense breath. "Are you certain of each of your commanders? Are they certain of everyone beneath them?"

"You're worried we've been infiltrated." Ysir narrowed his eyes in thought.

"Of course, I am. The King of Winter has been a masterful enemy so far. His plan is going well. No reason to believe he'd suddenly slack off."

"Don't forget the Gorgons and Medusa's two spawn," Auril spoke up. "It's possible some of the other dark gods are in league with them. Like the Furies or Harpies."

I started to tell her to hush, that speculation courted disaster, but I didn't. She was doing the right thing. Extrapolating the hell out of problems that might crop up. Better to be prepared than not.

"My daughter. I assume she remained with the dragons," Auril said.

"Why would she have?" Ysir glanced from Auril to me.

"Because she's finally broken through a barrier I constructed on the day of her birth," Auril replied. "Dariyah has claimed the other side of her parentage, and I believe she has wings. The dragons will teach her how to use them."

Auril was staring right at me, naked hope sheeting from her. I'd been planning to let Dariyah break the news, but I couldn't not answer, so I nodded.

Ysir's eyes widened. Wonder tempered with worry shone from them. "But 'tis the age-old legend come to life. The one that could spell Faery's ending."

Tears sheened Auril's silver eyes. "It is, and it means

my sacrifice wasn't in vain. For a long while I feared I'd interpreted the signs wrongly. I knew we'd get to this juncture, invaded and struggling to stand, but my daughter's role had yet to blossom."

"You birthed her knowing she'd challenge Pegasus?" I sought clarification.

Auril turned toward me. "Aye. I birthed her to save Faery from the dark gods. From the Gorgons and monsters. Why else would I have suffered Pegasus's seed. He is horrible, disgusting. But like all men, stupid when lust runs hot. He saw what he wished, a mortal lass, and took what I offered. If he'd done more than skim the surface, he'd have penetrated more than my body. He'd have recognized my glamour for the sham it was."

"Medusa knows about Dariyah now," I said. "Presumably, so does everyone else."

"She'll titrate the tale," Ysir said.

"Nay. She'll sit on it," Auril corrected him.

"That will only work until I blow her silence to bits," I growled. "The truth should drive a wedge between the King of Winter and Pegasus. Hopefully, one large enough to sever their connection."

"It depends," Auril spoke slowly. "One of the bitterest ongoing arguments between the King of Winter and me was my staunch refusal to bear his children. That I seduced Pegasus with clear intent to create one won't sit well."

"There all of you are." Titania joined us. "Does anyone have any idea where Oberon is? I've searched with magic and can't locate him here, but he's still alive. If he weren't, I'd know."

I nodded. "My take as well. Dariyah and I were talking about him and how everything built with his magic will wither once he's no longer here." I scowled as annoyance took over. "We decided he was onto the plot to oust him and had countermeasures planned for such a contingency."

A breathy sigh burst from Titania. "He certainly could have. Nothing wrong with his mind, but he's lazy."

"Aye, and he never cared for anyone who wasn't Fae," I pointed out. "Unseelie are scarcely Fae. He even viewed them as one step down from the other Sidhe."

"Awk. Never let one of them hear you say that," Auril tossed out.

It had amazed me no one took Oberon to task once he became more vocal about his bigotry, but much like me, they made excuse after excuse for him. "How'd your stealth visit to the library go?" I asked Ysir.

"Splendidly." He clasped his veined hands together. "Titania's been helping, and we've moved all the key scrolls and many of the lore books to a safer location."

"We were preparing to make another trip when you

returned. Between remaining warded and teleporting physical objects along with ourselves, each junket requires a great deal of forethought." Titania sounded pleased. It must be gratifying for her to come into her own, not always skirting Oberon's moods and edicts.

Salvaging our history was wonderful news, and most welcome in the midst of the grim aftermath from the Unseelie's world. The dregs from my trip there still dragged at me. Dariyah's wings were incredible, but their presence served as a reminder she'd be in the thick of things, directly in danger's path. It flew in the face of my overarching need to protect her. Yeah, right. I needed to get over that one, and damned fast.

"Gather your commanders," I told Ysir. "We will meet at dawn to discuss next steps."

"When will the dragons come?" he asked.

"I'm not sure."

"When will my daughter return?" Auril asked.

I didn't know the answer to that, either, but assumed it would coincide with dragons showing up. "When the dragons are done teaching her," I said. "Where are you keeping the library materials?"

"Come with me. I will show you," Ysir offered. "Anything in particular you're looking for?"

"On my way to get more." Titania took on a ruddy glow. She vanished before I had a chance to extend wishes for her continued safety.

I turned toward Ysir. "Aye. I'm hunting for long-distance spells, something we could employ to destroy the Unseelie colony without risking too many soldiers."

The librarian drew his bushy gray brows together. "I believe we have that particular scroll. If not, I'll prioritize bringing it back."

"Excellent. Thank you. I assume the King of Winter and everyone who was in Dubrova have moved into the field."

"You'd be correct." Ysir lowered his voice. "Tell me about her wings."

"They're silver and reach from her shoulders to past her waist. Once they began to grow, they came in quickly."

"Silver, eh? I'd have guessed they'd be white."

I stifled a groan. What was it about seers where they all spoke in riddles? "And that's significant, how?"

"Not sure it is, Regent. My first guess is her own power percolating with the winged horse's altered the appearance of his magic."

"Nay. It had to be my casting to keep them from manifesting until the time was right," Auril said firmly, followed by, "I shall see you in a few hours. For now, I'll be presiding over the Midnight Court. Tonight isn't an occasion for revelry, but simply being together has heartened Faery's people."

COURT OF THE FALLEN

Inclining my head, I murmured, "Thank you for holding court in the midst of our tribulations."

"How could I do less?" Turning, she walked briskly away.

I mulled over their different commentaries about Dariyah's wings. Genetics has always felt like so much mumbo-jumbo to me, whereas magic is a comfort zone. My vote went with Auril's explanation, but I'd be a fool to discount Ysir pointing out their color was a discrepancy and might be significant. Regardless, Dariyah was magnificent. I didn't want to pick apart any portion of her newly claimed power.

Ysir guided me into a modest cottage built of stones. I'd expected random stacks, but the books and scrolls were grouped in a way that made sense to him, and he went right to a bundle of scrolls and handed several tattered ones to me. They were so old, the vellum had yellowed and cracked in places.

"Thought I'd rescued these," he murmured.

"Thanks. I'll settle in and return them to the same spot."

The corners of his eyes crinkled as he smiled. "You know me all too well. If I might have your leave, I'll join Titania. These trips to the ruins of what used to be my library go far quicker with two."

"By all means. I'll see you soon." His words coincided with a spell, and he disappeared quickly.

He'd been correct about me knowing him well enough to reassure him I'd be a responsible custodian for the scrolls. Ysir kept track of the precise whereabouts of tens of thousands of volumes and documents in Drubrova's library, including who had what checked out. A corner looked inviting, and I settled into it after laying the pile of materials off to one side. My plan was to scare up something drinkable and begin reading so I'd be ready for the upcoming strategy session.

What I really wanted to do was hurry back to Fire Mountain to see how Dariyah's lessons were progressing, but she didn't need me hovering. The dragons had alluded to a ceremony to formalize our troth, but they hadn't offered details about anything, including its timing.

I fashioned a bit of magic into a seeking spell and was rewarded by a bottle of mead, presumably from Auril's stocks. Adequately fortified, I dug into the top scroll, blowing dust off its leaves. Hours clicked past. Ysir and Titania came and went, depositing their finds and returning for another batch. Ysir took care to place each item in a particular spot. I had a feeling he was restoring how Dubrova's library had been arranged.

Despite my mind wandering, I made decent headway. Between reading passages, I thought about Dariyah and Auril and whether Dubrova could be rebuilt without too much difficulty. I had a feeling the answer was no, and

COURT OF THE FALLEN

we'd be best served starting over, but Faery might have her own opinions about that. She'd been quiet. Surely, she recognized I'd returned, but the place I was linked with her remained quiescent.

The third scroll held a precise set of instructions for long-distance destruction, but required some level of proximity to set off the chain of events that would result in the Unseelie world imploding and folding in on itself while it crushed all its inhabitants. When Ysir popped back in, I said, "Hold up a minute if you will, and take a look at this."

He crouched next to me and scanned the place I pointed. My hands were filthy, fingernails crusted with dirt. In our old world, he'd have sent me scurrying for the washroom. After a few moments, he straightened. I offered him mead, and he drank deep before asking, "What would you like to know about Cthir's spell?"

I quirked a brow. "Sounds like you knew him."

"Quite well, except Cthir was a woman."

"Why am I not surprised? Women make better tacticians than men. I had you read that passage for two reasons. First off, how close would we need to be? Second, is there another world where we could set up shop to accomplish this?"

"Yes, but it's not quite near enough. The world where you found the Unseelie is riddled with a subterranean network of large caverns. For this casting to have a chance of success, you would need to seed it from one or more of them."

"But how would that work? Could the warriors escape in time? It looked to me like once the spell was launched, only seconds remained before it detonated."

"Careful timing would be required." Ysir nodded. "Whoever does this would have to have their teleport spell ready to go and ignite it on the heels of the other one."

I straightened my back amid a few creaks and pops and stood. "When Dariyah and I were there, leaving was almost impossible. If it hadn't been for the runes on the door of Titania's prison, we'd never have gathered enough magic to free ourselves."

Titania shimmered into view, her arms full of dusty tomes. She laid them carefully on the floor and came over to us. "I heard some of that. Do you mean the runes Dariyah deactivated a glyph at a time?"

"The same. When even our combined magic wasn't making a dent in getting us out of there, she nearly fell into the declination where the castle had been and remembered the runes and their latent power. She'd only disabled enough of them to allow you to walk free. The rest remained for us to work with."

Ysir was on his feet rustling through one of the stacks. "Got it," he crowed and hurried back brandishing a black leather-bound book. Setting it on a table, he thumbed through it and said, "Here. Read this part."

I bent over his shoulder and scanned a primer on runes and how they held power. I hadn't known they could be linked with the magic intrinsic to a world's core. Dawn wasn't far off, and I couldn't afford to spend hours teasing apart every nuance.

"Tell me if I got this right," I said. "The runes were linked to the castle and Titania's magic and the remote world's core." At Ysir's nod, I went on, "Even with Titania's magic not in play, they still drew power from the world."

"And from Oberon." Titania's tone was sour. "His power was the lynchpin that cobbled my imprisonment together."

We'd known he wasn't dead, but this was one more bit of proof. I locked gazes with the queen. "You think he's going to pop back up, don't you?"

She nodded. "By now, he's figured out the Unseelie planned to jettison him as soon as his usefulness to their cause ran its course. He'll be furious, and he'll lie through his teeth about what his intentions were all along."

I narrowed my eyes. "He'd be the perfect patsy, er warrior, to take the point blowing up that world."

"Aye." Titania's silver eyes took on a feral glow. "We

convince him 'tis a way to redeem himself and hold out the promise of perhaps salvaging his kingship."

"We'd potentially solve two problems with that approach," I said.

"We have no idea where he is," Ysir broke in, "or if he'd show the slightest inclination to put himself at risk."

"The other niggling issue is we haven't tacked down how to escape from that world quickly," I murmured. "It will take more than a single mage to cast and ignite this spell if I'm reading Cthir's instructions correctly. Even after Dariyah pulled power from the runes, it took a while before my teleport spell activated."

"What if they're linked?" Titania asked.

"What do you mean?" I replied to her question with one of my own.

The queen blew out a breath. "Runecraft was one of Oberon's pet projects. My bet is those runes were his, but he mixed in power from the Unseelie and Pegasus. Dariyah could access it because the winged horse sired her."

"All right. But I'm still not seeing how that will help our warriors leave with the speed they'd need to avoid being crushed along with everything else on that world."

Titania leveled a look my way that said I wasn't running on all cylinders. "What took time, dear boy, was harvesting the runes' power. If that were done first, mixed with the teleport spells ahead of time, they should take off like a well-trained racehorse. Dariyah is more than up to the challenge."

It was a sound idea until I got to the word should. What if it didn't happen? What if there wasn't sufficient power left in the runes to do jack? I kept my concerns to myself. "Let's go meet with everyone," I said. Absent Oberon as a sacrificial sheep, it left Dariyah and me to ensure our people got in and out of that place safely.

She'd be more than willing, but I wasn't. A lot of pieces needed to line up on the gameboard. One big unknown was what effect the dragons' mating ritual would have on her and me.

"She will do what is necessary," Titania said firmly. "She's my niece, and Auril's daughter."

Ysir nudged her. "Aye, my queen, but Cynwrigg is in love with her. No man sends his heart into the thick of danger if any other options can be found."

Titania eyed me. "You'll get over it. She has a job to do. So do the rest of us. Let's get to it."

I opened my mouth and shut it just as fast. No point in arguing. Nothing to argue about. Not yet. One thing was certain, though. If Dariyah was part of the team assigned to take out the distant world, I'd be right there next to her.

## 7

## CHAPTER SEVEN, DARIYAH

The flying part was phenomenal. I could have dipped and swooped and banked forever. I'd been worried the wings would be clumsy. Turned out they were only awkward when I was doing things other than flying—and even those were improving with the speed of light. I no longer had to consider their additional weight when I was walking. Running was a work in progress, but my need to move quickly was superseded by spreading my wings and vaulting skyward.

Yeah, I took to flight like baby ducks embraced water, so that part of my time with the seers didn't last long. Once they'd convinced themselves I wasn't going to tangle my wings together and fall out of the sky, they whisked me out of the arena to yet another part of the dragons' extensive underground cavern system.

"How big is this place?" I asked, followed by, "Do you spend most of your time down here?" Given a choice, I assumed any sentient creature wouldn't want to remain aboveground overly long.

"As big as it needs to be," Goren replied in true cryptic seer fashion.

"Most of us prefer to be outside," Brynn answered my second question. "The suns are glorious."

I shuttered my mind, but I bet he read incredulity in my expression. "Where are we going?"

"The library, and then back to the arena, but for a different purpose."

"Aye, we must prepare you to fight," Goren said.

"I already have some skill in that regard," I bristled. Geez, it wasn't as if I was a total neophyte. I'd had my share of scraps with everyone from mortals to mages—and always come out on top.

"Let me be clearer," Goren continued. "You've never faced an adversary like Pegasus before, and—"

"What makes you so certain I'll be facing him now?" I cut in.

"The prophecy," he and Brynn said in unison.

"'Tis why we're going to the library," Brynn went on. "So you can read it for yourself and begin to visualize yourself in its central role."

"Consider it an honor," Goren murmured. "We do not normally allow anyone except dragons into our lore collection."

Part of me, a pretty big one, came within a hairsbreadth of saying, "Thanks, but no thanks." I've always avoided putting stock in soothsaying. My aversion was likely a corollary of living with Mother and her endless scrying, but my preference was more of a "surprise me" approach. My patience for sifting through multiple versions of a future event that might or might not even happen was limited.

"Of course you want to read this for yourself," Brynn said. He'd obviously chopped straight through the mental warding I'd erected. Since it was nothing but a waste of magic, I shelved it.

"How long is this, erm, scroll?"

"Not terribly," Goren replied. "What difference does it make?"

None, except I wanted to get going. The sooner I returned to Cyn and the others, the sooner we could launch part of our project to reclaim Faery. I switched topics. "This troth-sealing ceremony, when do you envision it occurring?"

"More a ritual than a ceremony," Brynn corrected me.

"Aye, ceremony implies guests," Goren said.

I waited, but neither of them said anything else.

We'd entered some kind of side branch in the endless warren of tunnels. No longer moving lower, we walked quickly. I'd learned to cant my wings outward. It made for better balance and an easier gait.

"You didn't answer my question," I told them.

"The next time both of you are here." Goren shrugged his wings amid a rattling of scales.

I started to point out that might not happen before we plunged into battle, but thought better of it. The dragons seemed to believe it was important, but if it wasn't critical enough to tack down a time, I wasn't about to push it. Cyn and I had a bond. I felt the alteration in the weave of my power. I wasn't at all certain what the dragons proposed would make the slightest difference.

Either my escorts weren't paying attention to my thoughts, or I'd offended them. Neither said word one. The end of the corridor rose up to meet us. We walked through what looked like solid rock into a sizeable chamber lined from the dirt floor to a twenty foot ceiling with books and scrolls. What was it with magical races and their fixation with libraries? Unlike most, this one didn't feature tables or chairs. Or ladders.

Mother had brought a few choice source materials with us. Moving from place to place with one eye behind us hadn't been easy, yet she'd schlepped the tomes along.

Leaving them behind had never been a question. Where we went, they followed.

By contrast, I'd never owned a book. I'd borrowed what I wanted from libraries and worked out spells as I needed them. Occasionally, I sketched out the bones of them, so I didn't have to constantly reinvent the wheel. It had become easier with the advent of electronics. No need for paper, and I could store what I wanted to save in the cloud.

Goren spread his wings, flew to an upper shelf, plucked something from it, and returned to where I stood. Magic cascaded from the book with a cracked tan leather binding; so much power I felt it from several feet away. Powerful enchantment tickled the hairs on the back of my neck and thickened my throat. The dragon was clearly waiting for me to take the tome from him. He'd extended it toward me, but a sense of impending something-or-other grew. Not exactly doom, but I wasn't certain I wanted to taint my next actions reading something that had been penned a millennia ago.

By dragons.

It would color my actions, perhaps make me hesitate when what I should do was plunge forward. I've always relied on my instincts, and they were shrieking not to touch the bloody book.

Dragons had their own take on everything. What if this was a tactic to ensure I did exactly as they wanted?

They had a horse in this race too. While I might see Fire Mountain as an almost uninhabitable hellhole, they adored it. I crossed my arms beneath my breasts. "Tell me about Pegasus and why you expect me to challenge him to a fight to the death."

Intuiting I wasn't about to grab the book and settle in with it, Goren tucked it under a foreleg and clasped it to his gold-scaled chest. The chamber took on an interesting glow. I'd never sensed dragon enchantment as strongly. It resonated at a different frequency than Fae power because of the preponderance of fire in all their castings.

"You know the myth parts as well as we do," Goren said. "What you do not know is what happened after Medusa reclaimed her head. She retreated into Hell and lower still until she was completely alone."

"And there she remained," Brynn picked up the legend, "for millennia. None of us knew why she remained in seclusion for so long—or at which point she reattached her head."

"All the stories you know about Pegasus and his association with Bellerophon—like the fight with the Chimera—occurred while Medusa was out of sight," Goren jumped in.

The seers had a way of tag-teaming everything. They wove their words over and under each other in an easy way suggesting they'd always operated in this fashion.

"We believe"—Brynn was back—"Medusa forged ties with the dark gods during her hiatus. She and the other two Gorgons. The King of Winter may have entered the scene somewhere near the tail end of her sojourn beneath Hell."

"Or not," Goren said and nailed me with his whirling eyes. "Much of what we have said is conjecture. 'Tis why we wished you to read for yourself. Different eyes and minds sometimes come up with more fruitful conclusions."

I swallowed around a dry throat and pointed at the book. "It's not exactly calling to me. Rather the opposite. I don't think it's wise, and I'm going to stick with my intuition on this one."

The dragons exchanged a pointed look. Magic scoured me from feet to head and back again. It burned and stung, and I smelled singed feathers from my new wings. "Stop that." I infused my best effort at command into my voice, but the probe deepened. Too late for a ward.

The unwelcome examination vanished as quickly as it had arrived. "That's a relief." Goren spewed ash off to one side.

"What is? Do not do that again. It was unpleasant."

Brynn shuffled forward and dropped a foreleg onto my shoulder. "Apologies, but we had to make certain."

Fuck. This was exactly like trying to drag information out of Mother. "Of what?" I growled.

"Your latent magic is newly awakened," he said. "When our lore book gave you pause, and you refused it, we were concerned your father's blood might have risen to the fore and contaminated you."

It took a moment for the implication to sink in. "What? You're worried Pegasus was lying in wait in some distant corner of my psyche, and now has his claws—er, hoofs—into me?" Without waiting for an answer, I plowed on, "It's absurd. Mother is meticulous. She'd never have set something up where I'd fall prey to darkness the moment her casting broke."

"With all due respect to Auril," Goren rumbled, "she put that working into place an exceedingly long while ago. Things can change."

Always quick to ignite, my temper threatened to explode; I made a grab for it. As cautious as if I picked my way through a field of unexploded ordnance, I chose my words carefully.

Taking a few steps back, I clasped my hands behind me. "You view me as a child, and I suppose I am in your eyes. You also see me as a magical inferior. Our power manifests differently, but there are bound to be situations where what I bring to the table works better than your enchantments."

Now wasn't a time to pussyfoot around. I had to

establish a level playing field and realistic expectations. I hadn't been anyone's puppet since my early lessons in magic with Mother, and I wasn't about to begin now.

I exhaled sharply and continued. "It could be as simple as a mismatch of magics, but something about that tome feels off to me. Beyond that impression, I want to be free to make the best decisions I can and not be tainted by something that was penned in a different time.

"You said things can change. It also applies to whatever is in the legend or prophecy or whatever it is you want me to absorb. The knowledge might be helpful, or it might hold me back at a critical juncture while I ponder something when what's needed is action."

I rolled my shoulders straighter. "While I appreciate the honor you extended me by offering to allow me to read about a future-seeing that is finally coming to pass, I respectfully decline. In terms of battle techniques, I believe I'd be better served practicing with those I'll be fighting alongside. What if something you teach me forces me into the uncomfortable position of choosing between doing what's best for Faery's army or taking on Pegasus?"

"He is more likely to turn his charm your way and seduce you to his side," Brynn pointed out.

"Aye. By now, Medusa will have told him he has a daughter, but to keep it quiet. He will not want to fight you, but he will recognize you as a mortal enemy," Goren cut in.

"Which will leave him with only two choices," Brynn said. "He will do everything in his considerable power to lure you to his side. Only if he fails will he plot your destruction."

"Medusa will not agree with his approach," Goren added. "Her preference will be destroying you because she's canny enough to understand she'll never be able to trust you. Pegasus is everything to her. She never warmed to Chrysaor."

I'd been looking from one seer to the other. "Reading between the lines, what you're telling me is I need to jump on the offensive and do away with him before any of the rest of this has a chance to play out." The seers nodded, scales clanking in agreement.

"Our first task is dealing with the distant world where the Unseelie have set up a staging area," I reminded them. "We can't very well wage a war with the battalions arrayed around Dubrova Castle when all they have to do is open that infernal portal again and reinforcements pour in."

"Surely, you and Cynwrigg have a plan to address that," Goren said.

I leveled my gaze his way. "We only just tacked down the location, and then we had a hell of a hard time teleporting out of there."

"Why?" Brynn infused realms of significance into that one word.

I told him about the world changing from bucolic to something out of a nightmare and extracting residual magic from the runes. Both seers were surprisingly good listeners given my impression they regarded me as substandard on nearly every front.

"That's...interesting," Goren said when I was done.

"Interesting, how?" I didn't add this was an instant replay of my years with Mother where every bit of data had to be cunningly mined.

"More than Unseelie magic must be in play." Smoke puffed through Brynn's partially open mouth.

"As in?" I spun one hand in a circle.

"Perhaps you've located the other Gorgons, or a few of the dark gods. It would make sense they'd establish a residence near their troops to keep an eye on them."

I cocked my head to one side, debating whether to give voice to my thoughts, but either we were allies. Or we weren't. "It would help a lot to know more about who stands against us, and why. I'd find that far more useful than a prophecy set down a thousand years ago."

"Longer than that," Goren corrected me, "but your point is well taken."

"The why is simpler than the players," Brynn said. "Faery is a rich trove of potential power. Magic has been fading from all worlds for quite some time now. We here in Fire Mountain have guarded our gateways well. It's simple enough to do because we are aware whenever anyone breaches markers wrapping around our world."

"Those of you who lived in Faery—" Goren began.

"Not me," I interrupted. "I've spend my days on Earth since leaving Mother. Until recently, my mixed blood was a death sentence on Faery."

The seer rolled his spinning eyes; the effect was unique, adding to the mesmerism factor. "You're missing the point," he said emphatically. "Whether you were there or not, those who inhabited Faery have taken her for granted. Assumed their magical environment would always remain no matter what."

"You were also sloppy about keeping tabs on who came and went," Brynn added. "As I recall, you even invited humans into Faery for a while to strip them of their riches under the guise of providing a unique tourism experience."

"It wasn't me," I muttered, knowing full well that even if I'd been there, I wouldn't have objected.

"Anyway," Brynn continued, "while Faery waltzed along without a care in the world, others have eyed her riches and schemed to capture them."

"In order to do that," I said, "they had to make an end run and overtake Faery."

"Exactly," Goren agreed. "'Twas what your mother saw in her glass or her pool or however she gleans the future. A key element of scrying is the more times you see something, the more likely it will come to pass. Auril didn't prance off to seduce Pegasus until she was absolutely certain such a path was necessary."

"Do you know anything about which of the wicked gods are part of this?" I asked.

Both dragons shook their heads.

"All right. I need to get back to Faery. I want to be part of the planning process for our next steps."

"You cannot leave until we teach you some basic defensive maneuvers." Brynn skewered me with his whirling eyes.

I started to tell him I didn't need instruction in warcraft, but something about the way he was looking at me stilled my tongue. I'd already rejected the lore book. It wouldn't kill me to spend an hour flying around avoiding fire or whatever they were planning to toss my way.

"All right. Back to the arena we go." I tried for jaunty, but ended up sounding put upon instead.

The dragons' unique magic scooped me up. In the space between two heartbeats, we traded the library for the training arena. Both seers took to the air and rained fire on me. It was a solid wakeup call about how fast things can turn to shit.

Leaping skyward, I directed magic to douse the places my wings were smoldering from errant sparks.

Once I'd dealt with that danger, I skirted fire and ash while choking on smoke. Sometimes it was so thick, it obscured my adversaries. I've always seen myself as quick on my feet, but it took me so long to build a ward and deploy magic to determine where the dragons were, I ended up with holes in my clothes from cinders.

It shames me to admit a solid five minutes ticked by before I got my first shot off. If this had been real, not a simulation, I'd have been dead. That's the thing about humble pie. Either you let it choke you, or you suck it down and learn something.

Two hours later we were still at it. Ragged breaths ripped from my lungs; the muscles working my wings felt like blocks of lead. I'd be beyond sore after this. I wanted to ask for a break, but pride is a nasty taskmistress. I'd have fallen out of the sky before I requested mercy.

The world blurred into shades of gray, but I kept on slugging. Avoiding their shots and lobbing off ones of my own. One of the seers must have been trying to get my attention for a while because his voice finally blasted into my head.

*"Dariyah!"*

"Huh? What?" I peered through the smoky air and flapped wearily.

"Land. You need a break." Brynn had switched back to normal speech once he had my attention.

I did my best to spread my wings to break my landing, but fell to my knees when my legs didn't want to hold my body upright. Sinking into a heap, I sucked air into my lungs.

One of the dragons lumbered up to me. I should know which one, but my eyes had shut of their own accord. "Drink this," he rumbled.

I pried my eyes open and looked at a beaker full of bubbling golden liquid. "What is it?"

"It will strengthen you. I fear we kept you in the air too long for a first exercise."

I made a grab for the beaker, shocked at how tough it was to curl my fingers around it. Prepared for anything, I gulped from the flask. It tasted of fire and ash and flowers, not unlike aged spirits. By the time I'd emptied the beaker, my heartrate had slowed, and my breathing was better.

"You really should remain," Goren said.

"Aye, you could use many sessions like today's, but we understand why you wish to depart," Brynn spoke up.

I checked my magical reservoir. Not surprisingly, it was quite depleted. "Looks like I'm not going anywhere for a while, but I'm not going to be good for anything else, either."

"The brew is restorative. You'll be back to yourself sooner than you imagine." Brynn came closer to smiling than I'd have thought possible.

"Stay until your power is up to snuff." Goren took the empty flask from me.

"We will be in touch soon," Brynn said, and the two seers shuffled from the arena.

It was a relief to be alone. I reveled in the silence and simply sitting still until I had enough juice to teleport back to Faery. I hadn't meant to be gone this long. Rooting for the elixir—or whatever I'd drunk—to finish revitalizing me, I set a journey spell in motion. I needed to be 100 percent when I crossed into Faery—or close to it.

Who knew what I'd face. I had to be ready for damn near anything. I shook my head; the fuzzy feeling was clearing but not quickly enough. Just my luck. I'd finally found a man to grace my life, to love and cherish, and it could be months before we had any time to ourselves.

Or years. Or never.

Faery jolted into being around me. I'd aimed for a quiet corner of the Midnight Court's central glade. Good thing. The sounds of battle hit me like a wall before my spell was done unwinding.

The first thing I did was craft a ward. The second was follow my link to Cyn.

## CHAPTER EIGHT, CYN

I'd suggested Ysir invite his battalion commanders to the dawn gathering. Instead, he'd told everyone to show up. Strategically, it was better since it added more of a sense of ownership to whatever the group decided. I'd been concerned too many voices and opinions would prove unwieldy, but everyone was respectful. They understood full well Faery's fate balanced atop a razor's edge. We had to get this right. If we didn't our world, which was already in serious jeopardy, would be lost to us forever.

Ulane, one of two unicorns who sat on Faery's court, had been discussing efficient use of resources when an enemy had superior magic. With no warning, his head whipped around, lush white mane flying in the wind.

Head kicked back, he neighed briskly and took off at a full gallop toward the east.

At first, I figured he'd heard something and raced off to investigate, but all the other unicorns ran flat out to catch him. Augmenting my voice with magic to make certain everyone heard, I cried, "After them. We may have a chance to put some of what we talked about into practice."

Titania had intercepted two Unseelie spies on the eastern sector of the Midnight Court. I'd thought we plugged that particular weak spot. Not anxious to second guess anything, I sprinted across the green following the track where many unicorn hoofs had chewed holes in the verdant ground cover. Grunts, shouts, and howls buffeted me before I could see anything.

Ulane's instincts were solid, plus out of all Faery's citizenry, unicorns were the trained warriors. They practiced their skills from the time foals and fillies were weaned. Ysir moved with a sprightly aspect I remembered from his much younger days as he hustled everyone into battle formations.

Unseelie poured in from somewhere. Shit. Had they reestablished the portal to the horror of a world Dariyah and I barely escaped from? I was grateful she was with the dragons. At least she was safe. I bolted to the head of a company and shouted orders as I dug deep, calling on Faery to help me build a barrier and close the infernal gateway—if a new one had indeed formed.

I felt the link vibrate, but she didn't respond. I hoped it meant she was busy planning something that would be useful but didn't waste time perseverating over it. Magic came at me. So far, my warding resisted the barrage, but it flexed and bent before bouncing back and holding the next onslaught at bay.

The others in my company scuttled behind the ward, adding their magic to strengthen it. For some, the addition was noticeable, but for most not. I wanted to tell all the little animals and tiny faeries with their whirring wings to take cover, but they deserved a chance for valor too. Power doesn't always come in big packages.

The air thickened and crackled as dark Sidhe magic ran up against ours. Sparks flew, igniting everything they touched. Between Ysir and the unicorns, we'd formed ten companies, arrayed like the spokes of a ragged wheel. The unicorns hadn't bothered with warding. Probably got in the way of impaling whatever crossed their path. Their horns looked as if they'd been dipped in red paint. The rich copper scents of blood and the pungent stench of spilled entrails mingled into a noxious brew. Faery would do well to suck residual magic from the dying Unseelie to strengthen herself.

The sun inched up the sky as we clashed and clashed again. I hadn't heard from the land, and at this point I wasn't expecting to. Her absence pissed me off. What? Did she think she got a buy? That she could sit on the sidelines watching and waiting?

It didn't work that way, and I'd make certain she knew as much. At least she was unstinting as I mined for still more power and turned myself into a conduit as it flowed through me. Some I used to shore up my troops; the rest I lobbed at one Unseelie after another. I got better, more accurate, and sharper at judging exactly how much magic I needed to fell someone. I wasn't aiming for permanent death. The unicorns were taking care of that part. I immobilized Unseelie to make it easier for the unicorns.

Every time I glanced up, it seemed more stood arrayed against us. How could that be? We'd been fighting for hours and hadn't sustained too many losses on our side. Titania and Auril had taken over moving the wounded off the field, and presumably working healing magic.

If I hadn't been up to my eyeballs in carnage, I'd have noticed a familiar scent far sooner. As it was, Oberon's characteristic whiskey-and-musk stench hit me in the guts a split second before he sidled up and clapped me on the back. "Dear boy. You're doing a splendid job, but I'm back now, and—"

"Go fuck yourself."

"Show some respect." Still garbed in the richly

embroidered robes he favored, he drew himself up to his full height, which was several inches shorter than mine. His long silver hair had been woven with tiny jewels into hundreds of small braids. "I had a plan, son. One I've been working on for a long while now. As Regent, you have every right to feel miffed because I didn't include you in it, but—"

"Miffed doesn't even come close," I snarled and locked gazes with him. His silver eyes held a drawn aspect. He looked worse for the wear, but his patrician bearing hadn't altered.

"Aye, I'll apologize later. Once we're not up to our eyeballs in Unseelie scum. You'll see how brilliant my plan and execution are once I explain everything."

I'd have laughed at the absurdity of him believing any explanations could come close to making up for all the death and destruction in Faery, a land he'd been tasked to protect. His gaze turned from shrewd to speculative as he wondered just how big a fool I was.

He'd always underestimated everyone, me included. Mostly because he was convinced of his own superiority, he dished out hyperbole and swallowed it hook, line, and sinker. Nothing easier than believing how amazing he was—for him. The rest of us had seen through his bullshit long before he walked away.

I wasn't certain it would work because we shared so much blood, but I dropped the same type of weave over him I'd used with Aedan and held my breath. Would it contain him? Or would he break right through it? Absent his bond with Faery, he was weaker than I'd imagined. My cage turned out to be major overkill, but better safe than sorry. I had enough on my plate; the last thing I needed or wanted was to deal with his skanky ass.

*"Good for you,"* Faery's voice reverberated in my head.

She was finally in a chatty mood? Interesting. It suggested she'd known about Oberon's arrival and hadn't warned me. I wasn't any happier about that than the ex-king-in-a-cage pitching a fit. Ignoring both of them, I returned my attention to the battle. We hadn't lost ground, but neither had we gained any.

Oberon shifted from cursing to pleading with me to apologizing before returning to curses. I tried to screen him out, but he was a meter away, and it wasn't possible. An owl swooped close enough I sent him hunting for Ysir. We needed to figure out where our enemy was coming from. It was remotely possible all these troops had been arrayed around Dubrova, but I doubted it.

Had the portal opened again? Had they crafted another one? The more I thought about it, the more I leaned toward the latter. Surely, they'd sensed Dariyah and me when we'd landed on their world. Intuiting our intent, they'd grabbed the point and were running with it.

Strike first. Strike fast. Strike hard.

If none of us were left, their world would be safe.

"What the hell?" Dariyah's voice brought my head whipping around. I hadn't felt her approach. She slapped the side of Oberon's cage. "You old fucker. Best place in the world for you, eh? Dead would be better, but captured is second best."

"I returned to save Faery," he shrieked, showering the inside of the dome with spittle. "And you're no Witch."

"Took you long enough to figure that one out." Laughter rolled from Dariyah, harsh and bitter. At least it shut Oberon up. He wasn't used to overt displays of distain.

Ysir chose that moment to shimmer into corporeality. His eyes widened; a grin split his face. "Good one," he said and jerked his chin toward Oberon.

"Forget about him," I said. "There must be a portal."

"There is. I would have been here sooner, but I wanted to locate it."

"Did you?" Dariyah asked.

Ysir stared at her, taking her in. "Gorgeous wings, my dear."

"Why thank you. I'm still getting used to them."

"I know where it is," Oberon squealed. "I only stopped here as a courtesy before hurrying to close it off.

Faery isn't speaking to me. You must cede the land link now I've returned, and—"

"We altered the covenant," I told him. "You will never be king of Faery again."

"You can't do that," Oberon howled. "It's not within your power."

I dusted my hands together. "Signed, sealed, and complete. You cannot change the will of the people."

"You cheated. You lied to the court. You—"

Power flared from Dariyah's raised hands as she added a sound barrier to my cage. "Good call," I growled.

"You think? I'm sick of listening to him."

"Can you make it flow both ways?" Ysir asked.

"Sure." Dariyah added a few bands of enchantment and effectively sealed Oberon in silence. We couldn't hear him, but more importantly he couldn't hear us, either.

"Did any of the dragons return with you?" Ysir asked Dariyah. When she shook her head, he reminded us they'd sealed the last Unseelie channel.

We could call them, but I didn't want to embrace defeat before we'd even attempted to obliterate the hole ourselves. Repeating Dariyah's question, I asked, "Did you find the opening?"

"Aye. 'Tis better fortified than the last one."

Reaching for Faery was far from second nature, but

she was the logical choice for this task. The portal opened into her world. Assuming she'd been listening, I said, *"You know where the incursion is, right?"*

*"Aye, I do."* Her response was snappy enough, it gave me hope.

*"What do you need to close it?"* I asked.

*"Her body. 'Tis stronger than before."*

Dariyah, Ysir, and I exchanged a pointed look before Dariyah opened her own telepathic channel to Faery. *"No. After your abrupt departure last time, my body is off limits, but perhaps we can help you locate yours."*

*"After the gateway is shut,"* I tossed out so there'd be no mistaking my priorities. I had no idea how much of a production number it would be to locate and resurrect her corporeal form. If it were easy, she'd have done it long since.

Ysir narrowed his eyes. *"You do not require a body to seal the breach...my lady."*

I waited for a landslide or the earth beneath our feet to drop us into a chasm. Neither happened. *"It would be easier,"* Faery sniped, sounding put out.

My temper frayed, an angstrom from snapping. *"Apparently, you knew Oberon was here. You failed to alert me. You know where Unseelie are pouring into Faery killing your people. It is your duty as guardian of these lands to fix what you can without using every problem as a bargaining chip. Do I make myself clear?"*

I didn't care if she erupted in rage. I was done pussy-footing around because I was so grateful to finally have the land link in place.

*"Abundantly. I will, however, require an infusion of magic from Auril, Dariyah, and you."*

"Where would you like us to be?" I kept my question neutral, but I didn't trust her.

She sent a location blasting into my mind. It wasn't far from the shore of Faery's ocean next to an impressive band of cliffs.

"I'll find Mother," Dariyah said and took off running.

I tightened the weave of Oberon's prison. Leaving him where he was wouldn't hurt anything.

*"Send him to me."* Faery's tone dripped honey.

Intuiting she meant to drain him to bedrock, I said, *"If he's who separated you from your body, we may need him to locate it."*

*"Noted."*

Dariyah and Auril sprang forward. A corner of Auril's mouth twisted downward, and she wound her own layer of enchantment around Oberon's cage. "Exactly what you deserve, you craven fucker," she said.

"He can't hear you," Dariyah told her mother.

"Maybe not, but he'd have been better off taking his chances with the Unseelie. They might have found a use for him somewhere. Not going to happen with us."

*"I will exploit him until he's all used up."* Faery's voice filled the clearing. *"Now hurry."*

"May the gods look favorably on your efforts, Regent," Ysir said and bowed formally.

I'd take all the good wishes I could get. The teleport spell I'd begun to cobble together bloomed around us, and I swept us to the location Faery had indicated, keeping us well warded. Wise of me. This illicit portal was twice the size of the last one, and the King of Winter—or someone—had anchored it firmly into granite crags.

I felt Faery's impatience, and her power. I wanted to ask if she had a strategy, but she was already furious I'd shamed her. No one likes to run out of choices, and she was no different than the rest of us.

*"Tell us what you require,"* I sent in shielded telepathy. The last thing I wanted was to give our position away.

I expected a snide comment about her already making her needs known and being snubbed, but she didn't go that route. Perhaps the specter of having Oberon at her disposal had lightened her bleak mood.

*"Open yourselves to the land,"* she commanded.

I reached for Dariyah's power first, so we'd be joined. It should make it impossible for Faery to jump into her body, but I wasn't certain. This was war, and sometimes allies' demands required a leap of faith.

"We can do this," Auril said and joined hands with her daughter and me.

The second we established a channel, Faery mowed through us with a shocking display of strength. I'd thought her feeble. I'd been wrong. She had magic to burn when she wanted to employ it. The break carved into the cliff rumbled ominously. Fire shot from its maw, and it folded into itself. Boulders rained down, making the earth shake.

Some Unseelie who were in transit were cut in half. Blood coated the rocks, but not for long. Faery sucked it into herself; her impressive power growing quickly. Others who'd just emerged scrabbled for a way back. Absent their tunnel, they teleported away from Faery. Excellent. A few less warriors to deal with.

The serpents Ysir had sent to the sea crawled onto the shore. Between fire and magic, they made short work of the remaining Unseelie. I still had Dariyah's power in a solid grip. Faery could be sly, and she might execute an end run just when, assured of a minor victory, we relaxed our vigilance.

Auril chopped a hand downward, and our link with Faery vanished. Dariyah nodded my way. "Thanks." She didn't say she didn't trust Faery as far as she could see her, but she didn't have to.

*"Thank you for your efforts,"* I told Faery.

*"My thanks will be Oberon. Send him to the cave."*

I started to remind her he held the keys to returning her body, but she'd heard it once.

*"The King of Winter is withdrawing."* Ysir's mind speech held a jubilant ring.

"I heard that," Auril said. "Good news, indeed."

It was. It would offer us breathing space until the next onslaught.

The serpents moved among the fallen, chowing down on them. At least all that meat wouldn't rot and go to waste.

"Shall we?" I said.

"Aye, back to the Midnight Court," Auril agreed.

Dariyah's wings had been folded across her back. She fluffed them and jumped skyward. "See you there," she cried just before she vanished.

Auril looked after her for a long moment before wrenching her gaze from the skies. "She's beautiful."

"And deadly," I reminded the queen of air and darkness.

"That too," Auril agreed. "Today, we won. We must ensure it's the first of many victories."

"Easy words," I murmured.

"Nothing worthwhile comes cheap," she retorted, sounding like a cross between a mother and a queen.

A quick journey spell brought us out next to Oberon's prison. Between Auril and I, we packaged him up and sent him downward. Dariyah strode toward us. "Good riddance," she said.

"That one's like a bad penny," I told her. "If there's some sly way he can slide out from Faery's clutches, he will."

I left it at that, but I had a sneaking hunch he'd use her body as a bargaining chip for his freedom. Naturally, he'd promise to go far, far away, but his promises weren't worth the air it took to create them.

"We must leave," Dariyah told me.

"Where are we going?" I expected her to say back to Earth, but she surprised me.

"I heard from Ash. We're expected at Fire Mountain as quickly as we can get there."

## CHAPTER NINE, DARIYAH

F aery made a single attempt to slip into my body. It was so stealthy and so quick, if I hadn't been paying close attention, I'd have chalked the prickly sensation up to all the magic raining down from the broken portal. Something—probably Cyn's magic woven in with mine—sent her scuttling away. I hoped to hell she wrested the secret of where her body had ended up from Oberon. Once she had her own form, she'd stop lusting after mine.

The wings had to be a hell of a draw. We could fly now. Or I could, but I wasn't in a sharing mood. Despite my misgivings, the wings felt as if they'd always been a part of me. Maybe because they had even though I didn't know about them. Much as I valued Cynwrigg, the bit where I had to make love with him to unlock my full magical potential rankled.

It was stupid, too twenty-first century for words, but I'd have liked it better if I'd discovered my own path out of the morass of Mother's concealment casting. What was it she'd said? That she hadn't known what the key was, except I didn't completely believe her.

While she couldn't have seen Cynwrigg as the lynch-pin, she may well have intuited it would be some man who'd break down my barriers and shine light in the dark recesses of my psyche.

I'd chosen to fly to the Midnight Court—because I could and flight was still new enough I reveled in the sensation. Before I touched down, Ash's gravelly voice trumped into my mind. *"Return to Fire Mountain. Bring Faery's regent with you."*

The urgency in his sending was unmistakable. *"Did something happen?"* I sent back, not at all sure my own telepathy would stretch that far. Perhaps it didn't because he didn't answer me.

His message broke my concentration, and I didn't come out exactly where I'd hoped. Getting my bearings, I hurried to Mother's altar at one end of the Midnight Court's central glade and told Cyn we had to get moving.

"Not a bad time for you to take a small break," Mother said. "If they're willing, bring a few dragons back with you."

I turned to Cyn. "We should take a peek at the tent city arrayed around Dubrova."

He elbowed me. "You've been reading my mail. Are you certain you didn't command armies in an earlier life?"

"Quite certain." I laughed and added, "Immortals don't have 'earlier' lives."

"I shall spread the news of today's victory among the wounded. Some may be well enough to take advantage of tonight's revelry," Auril said and strode away.

I stared after her.

"What?" Cyn placed a hand under my elbow.

"Nothing. I feel torn, though. I should remain until all the wounded have been tended to, but Ash was quite insistent."

"Did you ask why?" Cyn raised a blond brow.

"Yeah. He didn't answer. I figured he couldn't hear me."

"Eh, he probably did."

While I was turning over what Cyn meant by that, his magic wrapped around me. Almost as familiar as my own, it made me feel protected. Yeah. Right. I needed to shelve the helpless female motif and bury it deep. Safety was an illusion, but I leaned into his enchantment anyway. Inhaling his familiar scents, I blended power with his. We emerged behind the castle. It was a good vantage point because no one appeared inclined to use that particular bit of real estate.

Not certain what I'd hoped for, I scanned unending rows of tents and other temporary structures. If anything, more of them dotted the courtyard both in and outside the gates than before. Unseelie were running this way and that. Some shouted orders. Others screeched curses. Apparently, they knew their reinforcement spigot had been clipped off at the roots.

I poured power into our warding. This was not a spot for someone to catch us spying on them.

"Part of their bitching is because they lost Oberon," Cyn whispered.

I focused my third ear, listening intently. Cyn was correct. The blame game was trickling downhill. Clearly, the King of Winter was looking for a patsy. Someone to string up as an example of incompetence. Movement overhead caught my attention. Pegasus, Medusa, and two other winged horrors were circling Dubrova's ruined turrets.

I hadn't let myself think much about the castle. Once a graceful structure, it had been relegated to a rubble heap that reminded me of Europe after World War Two. Nudging Cyn, I raised my gaze.

He gripped my hand so hard it hurt. "Stheno and Euryale." He barely breathed the names of the other two Gorgons. While I watched, riveted by a combination of

fascination and horror, riders shimmered into view on all three Gorgons. Hooded figures garbed in dark robes.

Cyn still had a firm hold on his teleport spell and whisked us away. "But I wasn't done," I protested.

"Aye, you were. Those were Shadow Lords astride the Gorgons."

My mouth dropped open. "How do you know?"

"I've had a run-in or two with them. Never forgot the particular prickle of their power. That they've joined forces with the Gorgons is unbelievably bad news."

I closed my teeth over my lower lip, thinking. "But you'd speculated they were part of this before."

"Heh. I certainly did, but I never expected it to materialize. No one's seen a trace of them for maybe a thousand years."

"We have to drive a wedge between the Winter dude and Pegasus." I nodded to myself. I was that wedge. The winged horse would recognize me as his get, and I'd make it clear Auril was my mother, and—

"You'll do no such thing," Cyn growled. "There will be a way to open the door to that truth, but we're not there yet."

Irritation curled my lip into a sneer. Before I blurted hot words, I forced a couple of breaths. Cyn loved me. He was taking care of me, protecting me. I couldn't fault him for that, but he had to leave me breathing room too.

"Do you think it will make a difference?" I asked.

"What? Knowing Auril birthed you?"

"Yeah. She staunchly refused children from the Winter King."

Breath hissed from between Cyn's teeth. "I'm not certain. It's been a lot of years. They may decide their alliance supersedes petty grievances because of a woman's whims."

"Mother is not just any woman." Defensiveness scoured me.

"To men like that, no woman rises to a level of significance," Cynwrigg pointed out. "Don't get huffy. It's one of those inconvenient truths."

"No duels to the death?" I looked askance at him.

"Maybe a few centuries ago, but probably not now. Too much is at stake. Think of all the planning that went into the siege on Faery. For the two principals to back off because of trivial jealousies seems unlikely. But I could be wrong. The King of Winter is a my-way-or-the-highway kind of ruler."

"So was Oberon," I reminded Cyn. "Look where it got him."

"Prepare yourself," Cyn muttered. "He might pull off sweet talking Faery into releasing him in exchange for her body. And we're nearly at Fire Mountain."

Nearly proved an understatement. On the heels of Cyn's words, the bake oven that was Fire Mountain surrounded us. Sweat poured from me as we settled on the burning, rock-studded sand.

Ash winged his way to us. "There you are. What took you so long?"

"We did a reconnaissance of the castle," I told him.

"After we shut a second portal to the Unseelie's world," Cyn added.

"How's Dubrova doing?" Ash asked, proving he was behind on relevant news, so I filled him in on Ysir blowing it up.

"The critical detail, though," Cyn broke in, "is Shadow Lords were riding the Gorgons. We left as soon as I determined what the robed figures were."

The dragon canted his head to one side. Fire shot from his open jaws along with ash and steam. "A pox on you for being the bearer of wretched news."

Cyn shrugged. "Would you rather not have known?"

"Of course not. Come with me." Turning quickly despite his bulk, he set a course for the cliffs leading into the underground cave system.

Questions zipped through my head, but I didn't ask any of them. Ash would tell us why we were here soon enough. We passed through winding corridors until we made it to the level where the dragons' meeting room was. Just as it had been my last visit, the cavernous space was full of dragons of all sizes and colors. I hesitated beneath the curved doorway, but Ash chivied us to the front of the room. My buddies, the blind seers, were there. Brynn and Goren raised forelegs in greeting.

"Stand there," Ash said gruffly.

I faced the assemblage with Cynwrigg on my right side, lacing my fingers with his. Elana, the healer who'd helped Mother hurried over. "Auril. How is she?"

"Fully recovered, thanks to you," I said.

"What made the difference?" the dragon asked.

No way to sugarcoat the truth. Either I didn't answer, or I gave it to her straight. The dragons had been generous with me, so I opted for the latter. "Titania broke through."

"Aye, but how?" Elana pressed.

"She, uh, might have slapped her a time or two and told her she didn't have the luxury of checking out."

The white dragon tossed her head back. Steam billowed from her open jaws as she laughed. "Whatever works," she trumpeted. "Whatever works."

Ash leveled a stern glance at her out of his whirling eyes. She nodded curtly in response and shuffled down one of the broad aisles winding between banks of raised platforms.

Before I could come up with a politically correct way to ask why we'd been summoned, Ash said, "You are here because war is upon us. We have a small opportunity to turn the tides, but we must act quickly. If we fail, Faery will be the first of many casualties."

Cyn gripped my hand tighter. Lines creased his forehead, suggesting he had a better idea than me exactly what that meant. I'd assumed we'd regroup, perhaps live in the parallel world of the Midnight Court for a while. If there were larger ramifications to the battle we'd lost, they'd escaped me.

"The Shadow Lords have risen," Brynn intoned—or maybe it was Goren. I still had the devil's own time telling them apart.

"Faery's regent confirmed as much," Ash growled. With his scaled lips skinned back from double rows of pointy teeth, he looked as if he could tear the world end from end.

Patience has never been one of my long suits. Rather than waiting around for explanations that might not materialize, I asked, "What does that mean, exactly?"

"It means—" Goren began.

Ash cut him off. "The short version."

"If I leave too much out, no one will appreciate how unexpected recent developments are," the seer protested.

"The only one who doesn't know the legends is Dariyah, and she'll figure things out," Ash retorted and snapped his talons, presumably to hurry things along.

Damn Mother all over again. She'd done a shit job of preparing me for any of this. Shadow Lords, whoever the hell they were, had received the most cursory of descriptions.

*"Because no one ever expected to see them again,"* Cyn's quiet voice ran through my mind.

Angling my head so I could see him, I didn't bother with mind speech when I said, "Bullshit. Mother knew. At the very least, she suspected my path would intersect with theirs. Or she'd never have gone to all that trouble to hide my name and my parentage."

"Quiet." Ash pointed a talon my way.

"Sorry," I muttered.

"The last great magical war occurred roughly fifteen hundred years ago," Goren said. "Grim and bloody, it spanned every magical world, all mages, and many years. Some magical creatures died out as did many worlds imbued with power."

Brynn held up a foreleg. "They didn't die out so much as they went into a type of stasis waiting for the proper combination of events to unfold."

"Aye, and they wait still." Smoke puffed from Goren's open jaws. "Dragons play a large part in what will happen next. Unfortunately, 'tis a role we neither solicited nor desired."

Irritation twisted my stomach into a knot. What was it with seers, anyway? Seemingly incapable of relaying stories in a linear manner, riddles were their métier, but we were running out of time. During the journey here, an impending sense of doom had taken root, and I couldn't shake it.

"Dragons must have played a large part in the last war," I said, hoping for clarification.

"We did," Goren confirmed.

"When it was over, we retreated to Fire Mountain determined not to repeat our errors," Brynn added.

Shy of screaming, "What errors?" I was out of options. Reminding myself I was a guest here, I clamped my jaws shut. Cyn could fill in the blanks, if any remained.

"You are in a hurry because you are young." Ash aimed his words at me.

I bristled. Young to him, maybe, but I was heartily sick of being viewed as a junior-grade mage. "Nope," I told him. "I'm in a hurry because we're balanced on the edge of a precipice. If we don't do something soon, we may as well not bother."

Cyn flinched at my brash words, but damn it, I hadn't cut my teeth around dragons. Before he did something that would really piss me off, like apologize for me, I kept on talking. "The whole time I was growing up, I sensed Mother had a grander purpose in her machinations. This"—I let go of Cyn's hand and spread my arms wide—"is what she sacrificed herself for. Whatever it is, let's get on with it."

"But the battle will be over you—your loyalties," Ash said.

"The markers are quite clear," Brynn added.

"It is why we worked with you to hone your skills." Goren puffed smoke upward. "And we did mention you were far from ready to leave."

"What did you mean about the battle being over Dariyah?" Cyn's tone could have etched runnels in granite.

Ash narrowed his whirling eyes and snared me in his unsettling gaze. "Your mother should have—"

"She didn't," I snapped back, too spun out to worry about being rude.

Fire flashed from Ash's mouth, missing me by a narrow margin. I shrugged. Fine. Pulling power into a hasty ward, I shrouded myself in it. I hadn't come this far to be immolated in dragon's fire.

"In Auril's defense"—Cyn's tone had shaded to neutral—"she did say you were slated to battle Pegasus."

"That's the barest beginning of Dariyah's undertaking," Ash growled. "Shut up, both of you, and listen. Before you leave Fire Mountain, you will have blended your essence—and your magic—with each other and with us. It is the only way we will have any chance at all."

While I was puzzling over who, exactly, we'd be up against if Pegasus was only the first of many, Brynn jumped into the explanation. "The last magical war ended because we sealed the Shadow Lords into what we hoped would be an unbreakable prison."

"Where was it?" Cyn asked, adding, "I never knew."

"No one did," Goren went on. "With some level of divine assistance, we built a vessel large enough to contain them and sent it into the ether eddying between worlds."

"Our handiwork held for so long, we quit worrying about it," Brynn said.

"Some of us may have," Ash broke in dryly.

Both seers swiveled to face their leader. Or king or prince or whatever he was.

"A particular constellation of events was spawned," Ash went on, "beginning with Dariyah's birth, and—"

"What if I'd never been born?" I asked. Not that I didn't want to be here, but if my coming along had produced all this, what in the fuck had Mother been thinking?

"The other alternatives were far worse," Goren said firmly.

"Aye, your mother chose a perilous road, but showed courage." Brynn's nostrils flared, smoke billowing from them.

"What were these alternatives?" I pressed. Ash had already said war could annihilate everything magical, so what could possibly be worse?

"We would have come to our current crossroads far

sooner, and without the benefit of your nascent magic to aid our efforts," Goren clarified. At least he'd answered me, and the reply hadn't been buried in puzzles.

"If you recognized the Shadow Lords were close to breaking out of their prison, why didn't you strengthen it?" Cyn pressed his mouth into a tight line.

"We tried," Ash said. "When Pegasus and the King of Winter formed an alliance, we grew concerned and broached the subject with Oberon."

"Let me guess," Cyn growled. "He glad-handed you, pretended to be interested, and did nothing."

"Exactly, so we withdrew to our own realm and hoped we were mistaken regarding the gravity of the situation." Smoke puffed from his mouth. "Dragons have always been an insular lot. It doesn't take much for us to write off the rest of the magical world."

I understood what Ash's warning about a short version meant now. A whole lot of rabbit holes beckoned. "Look here," they teased. "Fall through over there."

I'm not generally especially diplomatic, but I did my best to choose my next words carefully. "By the time you understood Oberon wasn't going to do anything, this particular train was too far down the tracks to derail."

Arching my brows, I looked from Ash to the seers. They didn't stop me, so I continued. "A long time before you reached that juncture, Mother saw...something a whole bunch of times and decided someone had to act. So she did. I was the result. What will happen once you do that binding ritual with Cyn and me?"

"And us," Ash corrected me.

"Aye, dragon essence must mingle with yours," Goren said.

I waited for more. They hadn't answered my question about the result of blending our various magics.

"We will form armies," Ash said. "Us, Faery, and every other magical entity from all worlds. Except, of course, those arrayed against us."

"There will be three battles," Brynn noted.

"Have you seen the outcomes?" Cyn asked.

"We have seen many outcomes," the seer replied, making me want to throttle him.

"What happened to sticking it out in the Midnight Court for a while?" I inhaled deeply and blew the breath out to center myself.

"Isn't that where you just fielded men?" Ash leveled his gaze my way, and I felt like an idiot. The Shadow Lords were loose and had signed on with the Gorgons and Unseelie. I didn't need to know more than that to recognize nowhere was safe.

"Glad you're on our side," I murmured. While I meant it, I was also hoping to redeem some of my earlier snarkiness. My tongue has sharp edges just like the rest of me. Being plainspoken only goes so far; I'd never exactly mastered diplomacy.

"We would have been content had this day never arrived," Ash said.

"We will fulfill our roles," Brynn and Goren said almost in unison. Turning, they blew fire on a phalanx of rush torches I hadn't noticed. The front of the chamber came alive with light.

Ash picked up a blade from a low table. "Hold out your hands."

Prickles marched up my spine. This was it. The place where the rubber met the road. Where my destiny, the thing Mother had sacrificed herself for, came full circle. Wishing I'd come from a normal family, whatever that was, was pointless. Normal families didn't birth mages. Cyn had walked closer to Ash, his left hand extended. I did the same.

"You are right to hesitate," Ash rumbled in his deep, gravelly voice. "Nothing will remain the same after this."

Cyn wrapped an arm around my shoulders. "I will still love Dariyah."

A thick spot formed in my throat. I swallowed around it and murmured, "I love you too."

Ash held the blade in one taloned foreleg and cut a quick gash in the other one. When his blood welled, deep crimson and smelling of fire, he chopped a gouge in the base of my thumb. His blood dripped into my wound. At first, I didn't feel anything but the pain of my injury, but then my hand grew warm.

Meanwhile, he'd mirrored his actions with Cyn's hand. "Press your cut places together," he ordered.

We did. What felt like tongues of fire shot from my palm up my arm. Once they hit my shoulder, they snaked through the rest of my body. Despite the relative cool of the cavern, sweat broke out on my forehead; my wings quivered.

Power words rolled from Ash. Stark and terrible, they filled me with dread and determination. Whatever this thing was, it was done; we'd cleared the first hurdle. Maybe dragon magic had always surrounded me, but it bloomed until it was dense enough to fill my nostrils and my lungs with their particular brand of enchantment.

"You are one with us," Ash intoned.

Cyn glanced over a shoulder and murmured, "No wings?"

"Check your magic," Ash sounded put out.

Cyn shook his head. "I was joking."

"Most of us have no sense of humor," Elana informed him, and I remembered how she'd laughed when I'd described Titania pestering Mother back to the land of the living.

I leaned into Cynwrigg and took the barest of moments to revel in the closest thing I was likely to have to a marriage ritual. There hadn't been any of the common human words, the ones about sickness and health or till death do us part. None of those concepts were relevant for immortals, but my bond to him had intensified until it felt unbreakable.

And then I understood it meant we would flourish or fall together. Disaster for one would spell the same for the other. I drew myself up tall. We'd come through this —both of us—no matter what it took to make it happen.

The dragons were shuffling out of the meeting room.

Cyn inclined his head at Ash and the seers. "Thank you. We shall return to Faery now and be in touch soon."

"You aren't leaving. Not quite yet," Ash informed him. "You shall train with the seers. Once they are satisfied with your skills, we will allow you to depart."

"Allow?" Cyn raised both brows.

"It's okay. Come on," I said and followed the seers from the chamber with Cyn walking next to me. He'd tripped over the word *allow*. I had too, but we'd talk later when we were alone. Meanwhile, I wanted to soak up every single bit of knowledge I could. I was a scrappy street fighter, not a warrior.

"Got to fast-track our skills," I murmured.

He made a grab for my hand. I squeezed hard, and we broke into a run to catch up with the dragons.

## CHAPTER TEN, CYN

I lost track of time while we worked through a series of military drills. Being the only one of our quartet without wings was quite the impediment. I'd only been half joking about not having any after the ritual binding me to Dariyah and dragonkind. I had my magical blade, the one capable of many forms, but it wasn't a substitute for being able to take to the air.

Food and drink materialized a couple of times. The beverage was some kind of golden bubbling concoction that made me feel heady and invincible, as if I'd snarfed a few lines of coke.

During one of our few rest breaks, Dariyah asked, "Do you suppose Faery is done slicing and dicing Oberon by now?"

"What do you mean?" Brynn fired off the question. "Did he return to Faery after all?"

A bitter laugh rolled from me. "You could say that. He showed up, swatted me across the back, told me I'd done a fine job as regent, but I could step down because he'd returned."

"Fascinating. How'd he end up victim to Faery's questionable mercies?" Goren shuffled close, a flagon of the golden beverage clutched in his talons.

"I didn't have time to listen to his crap, and I don't trust him, so I dropped a cage over his body."

"Later, we fed him to Faery," Dariyah said.

"Not the wisest move," Brynn growled.

"She requested we hand him over," I clarified. "Refusing would have been difficult."

"Aye. Understood." Scales clanked as Goren bobbed his head.

"Faery would ask for him. Their relationship has always been complicated," Brynn muttered.

I almost asked what he meant by that, but we'd already been absent from Faery for longer than I'd expected by a factor of many hours. I bowed briefly and asked, "When might we return to Faery?"

Dariyah fluffed her wings before folding them tight against her back. "Not that we don't appreciate the instruction. I need all the help I can get, but we didn't leave things in a particularly stable condition."

Power flickered around the seers. I figured they were engaging in a private form of mind speech. Dariyah and I passed a flask back and forth as we waited, but I'd made up my mind. If the seers indicated we had to remain, they'd get pushback from me.

Not only did I need to check on Faery. I also needed to drop in at Lady Luck to make certain the casino was still standing, and my employees hadn't taken advantage of my absence to run the till down to nothing.

Brynn studied us with his unsettling gaze before blowing a plume of smoke upward. "We would prefer you stayed, but to train you fully would require months."

"As an alternative, you shall return every few days for another session not unlike today's," Goren said.

Recognizing a compromise, I grabbed it by the short hairs but sought clarification. "No particular schedule? Just when we can get here?"

"Aye, or we will come to you. While we've been working together, the other dragons have mapped out a plan for who will travel to Faery. We must train with troops there and other mages we scare up from distant locales."

I'd been hoping for as much. One of our obstacles in the battle we'd lost had been a lack of just such preparation. Slapping folks together, particularly people like those who inhabited Faery, and assuming they'd become a sleekly oiled machine by osmosis, was absurd.

"We very much appreciate the support," I told them. "Please convey my thanks to Ash."

"He will not be pleased we released you so soon," Brynn mumbled amid clouds of smoke.

"Thanks for everything." Dariyah extended a hand upward; both dragons clasped it.

Before they changed their minds, I walked toward the entrance to the chamber. Dariyah joined me, and we hurried up winding passageways, aiming for the surface. We didn't pass any dragons along the way, but once we emerged into the blinding light of Fire Mountain's twin suns I understood why.

Dragons stretched as far as I could see. Some had initiated battle maneuvers on the ground while others fought from the air. Smoke, fire, ash, and steam wafted everywhere.

"They're taking this seriously." Dariyah pitched her voice low. I felt her gather magic to transport us away from here.

"They've always been warriors," I told her and added power to her spell. Maybe it was my brand-new link with the dragons, but Fire Mountain's heat wasn't as oppressive as usual.

"I've been thinking about that," she said as the dragons' world dropped away, traded for the cool darkness of a teleport channel.

"What in particular?" I asked.

"Many of Faery's people—and all the animals, especially the smaller ones—are vulnerable. Surely, we can assign them something that mitigates their danger."

"Before we go there, what'd you think about today's session?" I asked her.

"I've trained with them before," she reminded me. "They're harsh, but fair. They push you hard, but not so hard you fail. How about you?"

"I'm jealous. I want wings."

"You did okay on the ground," she countered. "I want a blade like yours that folds up to a pocketknife."

"Trade ya?" I dropped an arm around her shoulders, feeling the brush of feathers against my skin.

"Um. Nope. The wings are here to stay. I'm sorry I didn't know about them sooner. Speaking of which, I plan to have a chat with Mother. I figure she knows about the three battles, and I'd like to get her take on them."

"While you're doing that, I'll check in with Faery."

"You want to see what she did with Oberon."

"You bet I do." I snugged her against me. "If he's still in the wind, we need to know about it."

Our combined efforts were a real powerhouse. The Midnight Court shaped up around us far sooner than I'd have expected. Night was falling, and the glade was empty of wounded. If magic is going to heal, it works quickly.

Auril loped toward us. "Been keeping an eye out for you. It's been a while since you left."

"The dragons had their own agenda," I told her.

Power sparked down my body, and she cocked her head to one side. "I see. You and my daughter are joined, but I sense dragon in the mix."

"You knew something like this was afoot," Dariyah said.

"Of course I did." She clasped her hands behind her. "All has been quiet here. Ysir and the unicorns have been working on skills with those who are strong enough. The others are recovering, and we built fires to ease the dead to their next life in the *Summerlands*."

"How long before the next confrontation?" I asked.

She shrugged. "I wish my foreseeing worked like that."

"The dragon seer said there would be three battles," Dariyah said.

Auril nodded but didn't add anything. Dariyah ducked from beneath my arm and folded a hand around her mother's wrist. "I want to know everything you do about them."

"Not realistic. It would take too long."

"I have time." Dariyah let go of Auril.

It was a good opportunity to leave and let them hash things out. Common ground that would establish them as equals in Auril's eyes was a work in progress. After clearing my throat, I said, "I'm going to have a chat with Faery. I'll return as soon as I can."

Dariyah gave me a quick hug. "Maybe we can manage a speedy visit to Earth after you're back."

"Exactly what I had in mind. If we can work it in, we will." I held her close before reluctantly letting go. If I had my way, we'd never be separated, but those were the thoughts of a besotted fool, not Faery's regent.

"Join the Midnight Court later tonight," Auril urged. "It will do the people good to see their regent—and his consort."

I waited for a snide side comment about the consort part of things, but Auril smiled benignly. Perhaps she was warming to the idea of me as a son-in-law. More likely, when she'd prioritized all our problems, Dariyah and I had sunk to the bottom of the heap. I gave myself a swift mental kick in the backside. If we lost the series of upcoming battles, nothing much else would matter. One of the ramifications of being joined to Dariyah was we'd share each other's fate. That unsettling conclusion had come to me while we were mock fighting in the dragons' arena.

Had it been just her and me, we'd have been more like other mated couples—rare as they were. The addition of dragon magic in the binding altered everything. We'd prevail or sink together, along with any dragons who happened to be nearby.

I hadn't wanted to take chances with Dariyah before, but this added a whole new layer of complexity. Neither of us could afford to attract undue risks, yet we had to. I'd be leading the charge. As regent, my place was at the head of a column of warriors. Her fate hinged on the outcome of a battle with her father. I'd help as much as I could, but that confrontation would be an aerial one. If the Gorgons entered the fray, we'd counter with dragons.

Would it be enough? Or would we need to tap a couple of deities, assuming we could find them.

"Cynwrigg?" Auril's tone suggested it wasn't the first time she'd called my name.

"I'll be at the Midnight Court if I can," I told her and launched a spell to take me to the crystal cave deep beneath Faery. I wanted to check on Dubrova, but I'd do that on my way back.

The feel of Faery's magic intensified in the place I was linked with her. I took it as a good sign, one she was starting to believe in her innate power again. The cave was empty, but she'd know I was here. I hunkered down to wait, not forever but I'd give it a while.

So long as I had time, I scanned for Oberon's skanky presence. He'd certainly been here. Dregs of his essence remained scattered about. Rather than the sweet scents of good magic, his held undernotes of rotting vegetation and roadkill. Maybe I'd underestimated Faery, and she'd actually separated body from soul and done away with the liege who'd hogtied her and made her life hell.

After I wrenched my attention away from what was hopefully Oberon's remains, I tossed a seeking spell in a wide arc, not hunting for anything specific but checking the integrity of Faery's underpinnings. It was a low priority, but I wanted to rebuild Dubrova, restore the structure to its former glory.

I pushed myself upright with strict admonitions to focus on getting the Unseelie out of Faery. If we couldn't accomplish that, nothing else would fall into place, either.

"I know you're here somewhere," I said after it was clear Faery wasn't going to come waltzing in. "My time is limited, and we must talk."

A swishing sound was all the warning I got before a tall, patrician figure garbed in deep-purple robes walked toward me. It had to be Faery, restored to her body. I'd never seen her in this form, but back in those days I wasn't regent, either. Soft light shimmered around her, illuminating hair of gold and silver flowing down her back. Her eyes were like mine, a mix of metals that shone in the muted light of the cavern. I'd imagined her slender, wispy, insubstantial. The reality was a woman nearly as tall as me with broad shoulders, a strong jaw, and sharp cheekbones.

I narrowed my eyes. "You are whole again. Where is Oberon?"

Faery flapped a hand my way. "He'll not bother us."

My jaw tightened. I pried it open long enough to ask, "What makes you believe that?"

"You do not have the right to question me." A mage light bloomed in soft violet tones near her shoulders.

"We are allies," I pointed out. "Secrets among allies aren't wise."

She ignored my comment. "You were seeking an audience. What did you want?"

"Mostly to assure myself Oberon was out of the way. He will be a problem the next time he resurfaces."

"There won't be a next time." Faery arched both golden brows and looked askance at me.

I debated my next words, but not for long. "Don't be so sure about that. The other side has clearly jettisoned him. Titania won't give him the time of day. Auril would just as soon kill him as look at him, but the Oberon I remember lives for challenges. He will seize any opportunity he can, leverage any chinks in whatever armor you encased him in, and show up to make you sorry you traded his freedom for your body."

Faery stalked closer until only about half a meter separated us. Glaring at me, she said, "I am the land. You are merely regent, not a king. You serve at my pleasure. Remember the blood bond you swore?"

I remembered it well, but wasn't inclined to retreat into silence. Rolling my shoulders back, I faced off against her. "Dariyah and I are bonded with each other and dragonkind. If you sever my connection with you, we may not bother fighting the Unseelie to preserve you." Turning on my heel, I shot, "Think about it," over one shoulder.

"You wouldn't dare abandon me," she screamed.

"You're who brought up my oath. If you call it due, watch me." My temper is slow to react, but fury streamed through me. There'd been a time I'd felt sorry for Faery, been sympathetic to her plight when Oberon had hung onto the land link while separating it from Faery's citizenry.

No more.

I'd allocated sufficient effort to establish my allegiance, my devotion to what I'd assumed was a shared cause. Initially, it had been moving Oberon out of the way permanently. We could have done that—if she hadn't let him go. Since a dragon-constructed prison had proven inadequate to contain the Shadow Lords, anything she'd cobbled together to hang onto Oberon was certain to fail.

I made a grab for my equanimity as I stormed upward, bypassing a teleport spell in favor of simple movement. Faery was beginning to appear as self-serving as Oberon. No wonder the two of them had gotten along. Remembering my promise to take a peek at Dubrova, I cloaked myself in invisibility and drew my power in close.

A slight course correction brought me above ground at my favorite vantage point behind the castle. No more worries about being spied from a window; they were all smashed, the shards scattered on the ground, but the Unseelie would be idiots not to post guards. They'd lost the last round; losers tended to be vigilant.

The King of Winter must be incensed by his troops' poor showing, probably as angry as I'd been in the face of Faery's indifference to the gravity of our situation. She honestly believed she'd taken care of Oberon. Her annoyance with my questions had been genuine, but why was her memory so damned short?

Oberon had used and abused her just like he had the rest of us. I had enough foes riding me; I did not need another forcing me to constantly peer over one shoulder.

The courtyard within the castle's gates and the green on their far side teemed with activity. If the Unseelie had been inclined to leave, it wasn't apparent. Maybe the only ones to decamp had been those near the sea where we'd shut the portal. Tents and other temporary struc-tures dotted the land like a metastatic cancer. Pegasus and the Gorgons flew overhead.

Where were the Shadow Lords? I'd have liked it better if I could see them. Were they even now shutting off all access to Faery? It was what they did: closing off worlds and taking advantage of their isolation to conquer them.

Had Faery cut a deal?

Was it why she was so haughty and unapproachable?

I pinched the bridge of my nose between thumb and forefinger. We'd had a spat, but it was no reason to label her a traitor. No one bargained with the Shadow Lords. No one sane, anyway. I moved quickly, sticking to the perimeter between the edges of the encampment and the dying trees. The more I could find out, the better prepared we'd be. The Unseelie must have wounded, but I couldn't locate anything like a field hospital.

Perhaps they'd moved them elsewhere—or done away with them. The weak were a liability. I made a full transit of the area around the ruined castle. Dusk had fallen as I skirted the Unseelie camp, but there weren't any fires, nor did I smell food being prepared.

Had they not brought supplies with them?

It would be very like the King of Winter to assume Faery would fall without fanfare, and they wouldn't need anything much. I'd gathered all the information I could and was preparing to leave when I felt a tug on the link I shared with Dariyah. She must be near, but I didn't dare raise either my mind voice or my normal one. So far, no one had noticed me.

I wanted to keep it that way, and I certainly didn't want to draw attention to her.

Sure enough, she strolled toward the front of the castle as if she had all the time in the world. She must know I was here, but she didn't so much as bat an eye my way.

What was she doing unwarded?

I risked telepathy, shielding it as deeply as I could. *"Leave,"* I exhorted.

*"Remain hidden,"* floated back to me.

Like fuck I would. Tossing caution to Faery's winds, I bolted to Dariyah's side, shedding my warding as I went.

"That was stupid," she gritted without looking at me.

"Not any dumber than whatever you're doing," I shot back. "Whose idea was this?"

"Mine." She did glance my way then, her face carved into a mulish expression that told me more eloquently than any words the barn door was open and the cow long gone.

Dariyah hustled forward. Augmenting her voice with magic, she shouted. "I would parley with Pegasus and the King of Winter."

"Parley away," Pegasus whinnied from above as he circled to land.

"Aye, but don't expect to leave afterward. Either of you." The King of Winter walked through a gash in

Faery's ether and inclined his head my way. "Top of the day, Cynwrigg. It's been a while."

His unearthly beauty hadn't changed with the passage of time. Dark brown hunting leathers— breeches, tunic, and shirt—clung to his muscled frame. Rich auburn hair had been braided against his head with tiny, sparkly jewels. Slightly taller than me with a square jaw, high forehead, and chiseled cheekbones, he oozed hubris. Rings set with ostentatious gemstones circled most of his fingers, and lace-up boots graced his feet.

"We'll see about the leaving part." Dariyah tossed her head and faced the winged horse squarely once his hoofs touched down. Compulsion wound through her next words. "Look at me," she commanded. "What do you see?" In case there was any doubt, she bit into the end of one finger and blew on her blood as it oozed out.

The expression on the horse's face shaded from amusement to horror to something I couldn't interpret. "Impossible," he neighed.

The King of Winter had snaked out a hand and captured a droplet of blood. After smelling it, he tasted it. His striking features morphed into a mask of fury, pale skin reddening as he drove a fist into the horse's flank. "You. You're her father. You fucked my consort."

The horse fanned his wings. "Not knowingly. The bitch must have tricked me, and—"

"Our work here is done." Dariyah smiled sweetly,

grabbed my hand, and swept us into a spell she'd had at the ready.

"That was gutsy," I muttered. "Wish you'd have run it past me."

"Why? You'd have said no, and I'd have done it anyway. My spell will take us to Earth. Any objections?"

"None at all." Grim laughter rippled through me as I made certain no one could track us. "Glad you're on my side."

"Wouldn't have it any other way. Do you suppose Lady Luck will stand us another meal?"

"Maybe. Depends how your luck is running."

Her laughter joined mine. "Pretty strong, I'd say. Let's not jinx things by dissecting it."

I nodded agreement. Telling her about my argument with Faery could wait until after dinner. "Why were you so certain that would work?" I asked as the stairs beneath the casino came into view.

Dariyah shrugged. "Don't take this wrong, but they're men, aren't they? They may kiss and make up, but not before they do a whole bunch of dick waving."

The visual made me snicker. "Let's hope for a protracted pissing contest before they declare détente." Tucking a hand under her arm, I started up the steps.

"Sounds good on my end. We can't be gone long. Mother and Titania are planning another war council tonight at the Midnight Court."

"Did anything happen while I was talking with Faery?"

"Yeah, but it'll keep until we've eaten."

Curiosity jabbed me, but I sheathed it. If the crones were on the edge of launching the first of the three battles, I'd find out soon enough. The timing was ripe, though. Nothing like hitting hard when the enemy was in a state of disarray. Judging from the Unseelie king's response to Dariyah's disclosure, it would take him a while to focus on anything other than his scorched ego.

## CHAPTER ELEVEN, DARIYAH

I hadn't told a soul before I snuck away to toss my parentage in Pegasus's horsey face. Mother and Titania would have had the same reaction Cyn did. They'd have forbidden me to act, not that I'd have paid their injunction any heed. They did have the power to hobble me, though. Maybe.

Whatever the dragons had added to the mix of magics simmering through me strengthened my power dramatically. Whether I was a match for my mother and aunt was an unknown, but the simplest course was to slink off and take care of business.

I'd been surprised to find Cyn skulking around the castle, but not so surprised I was willing to abandon my mission. When he'd traded caution—and his warding—for open support, I could have hugged him.

I'd still do that, but it had been more important to toss my hand on the table and skedaddle out of there. I'd figured on the Unseelie king's outrage and hurt feelings. Always gratifying to know I've read a situation right. His anger offered me just the window I'd hoped for, and I unveiled the transport spell I'd held at the ready.

Maybe the rest of this war would go better than Mother assumed. If I'd been the Winter King, I'd have dropped some kind of snare over me the second I showed up. And I'd have widened it to accommodate Cyn. Not that either of us would have stood around and quietly let them fuck us over. We'd have fought back, swift and sure, but it would have blown a hole in my "get in, strike a blow, and get out" strategy. I hadn't done a whole lot of planning, but I had considered what I'd do if they tried to corral me, and it wasn't pretty.

I'm more of a scrappy street fighter than a tactician. In this case, I'd have spread my wings and leapt skyward before anyone had a good hold on me. In addition to my journey casting, I had defensive magic at the ready, and I'd have plowed it into everything I could see. All the while taunting Pegasus to figure out who I was.

Cyn had bemoaned not having wings, courtesy of our new connection with dragonkind. The part I wanted was fire. It would be fabulous to shoot flames at everyone who pissed me off.

I hadn't even needed my prepared defenses; fire would have been overkill. This time. Mother and Auril were in full agreement we needed to strike while the iron was hot, which meant rallying everyone who was well enough to fight and marching before dawn.

I'd sent a message to Ash. Hopefully, it went through. Dragons were a lynchpin. In light of the Gorgons and Shadow Lords, we needed a serious edge. If I didn't hear back from him or one of the seers, maybe we'd have to make a quick trip to Fire Mountain before the night was out.

Halfway expecting more pushback from Cyn, I was grateful he backed off after his comment about running things past him. We hurried through dinner while he checked in with a running cavalcade of casino staff. Word he'd returned spread like wildfire, and everyone wanted something. Happy for a respite when I didn't have to do anything except eat, I did my damnedest to clear everything related to Faery and the Unseelie from my mind.

I failed, but at least I slowed the traffic roaring through me from a major freeway with a bazillion lanes to a two-lane back road.

Cyn had left with someone who was insistent about showing him something. I was just considering if I had a few moments to check on Midnight when he tromped back into his office. Picking up his plate, he shoveled the remaining food on it into his mouth.

"Looking like it's time to leave," I murmured.

"Aye, before someone else shows up." He set his plate aside. His glamour flickered, and the tips of his ears poked through for a minute or two.

"What was the last problem?" I quirked a brow.

"Eh, we have a major plumbing leak on the north side of the basement. It's been an issue for a while, and we've been patching it, but that part of the system needs new piping. I authorized calling a contractor and getting it done."

"Can you hire someone to run things when you're not here?"

"Not easily. Finding someone who wouldn't redirect a chunk of the money flowing through Lady Luck to their own benefit is tough. There are casino management firms, but they all require an obscene percentage." Cyn crooked a finger my way. "Come on. We'll make a quick stop to look in on your cat. You can catch me up on what's happening, and I'll tell you about my chat with Faery."

His tone was a dead giveaway. "That bad, huh?" I stood and walked to where he stood. "She let Oberon walk?"

"She did, indeed. But the good news for you is she has her body back."

Cyn's spell snapped me up, and we traded his office for my flat. Midnight wasn't there, so I went to the window and whistled. He wasn't exactly a dog, but it might work.

"Faery has a long memory. She won't forget me turning her down," I murmured.

"Maybe not, but this will give her impetus to move past it." He drew his brows into a thick line. "Wish I was certain which side she was on."

Alarm sluiced through me. "Come on." I snapped my fingers. "You have to say more than that."

"Nay. Probably best if I don't. I'm buried in conspiracy theories, and they might not be much more than dusty imaginings."

Gliding to his side, I wove my arms around him. "I trust my instincts."

"It's easier to do that when you know the person involved. My bond with Faery is so new the ink's not yet dry."

Midnight streaked through the window and clawed his way up my body. I gathered the cat into my arms and stroked his matted fur as he settled into his steam engine imitation. Holding the large feline, feeling his purrs in the pit of my stomach, reduced my frantic need to micromanage every last detail, most of which I had zero control over.

"He's not done, you know," I said and sank to my haunches with my back against a wall.

Cyn crouched across from me. "Oberon?" at my nod, he went on, "I agree we haven't seen the last of him, but he's become a man without a country. His erstwhile allies made it abundantly clear they were using him. Faery views him as a traitor. At least, I hope she does."

"Not enough pretty words in the universe to smooth all that over, huh?" Midnight snuggled in deeper.

"Probably not, but his silver tongue still worked well enough to sweet-talk Faery into giving him his freedom."

I considered what it might mean. "Are there other places he might rustle up aid?"

"Beyond the *Dreaming*, which is now closed to him?" Cyn rolled back on his heels until his butt touched the carpet.

"Um, yeah. I thought Faery didn't have control over the *Dreaming*."

"She doesn't, but Ysir knows the gatekeeper. Once he understood the problem, he wove some kind of enchantment that would alert him if Oberon crossed into the *Summerlands*."

"One problem down." I'd have dusted my hands together, but they were full of cat.

"Aye. I'll take any victories at this point. Oberon could pose a problem, but he's not high on my hit list. Tell me what happened in Faery before you left." A corner of his mouth twisted into a wry grin. "I'm assuming neither Auril nor Titania were privy to your visit to Dubrova."

"Ya think?" I smiled back. "Mother, Auntie, Ysir, and the unicorns are all on the same page. They want to engage the Unseelie in another confrontation immediately. Something about riding on the coattails of our last win."

"It's a reasonable plan—so long as we win again." Cyn pushed upright, went to the sink, and sluiced water over his hands and face.

"Why wouldn't we?" I demanded.

"Never underestimate the enemy," he said, his words muffled in the paper towel he'd grabbed to dry himself.

"But they just lost," I reminded him.

Cyn dropped the wad of paper towels into a trash bag and put everything under the sink before digging a can of kitty food out of a cupboard. "They did, but they haven't exactly been sitting around on their asses wringing their hands. They're planning their next strike too."

"They were," I pointed out. "Now they're engaged in a pissing contest." Midnight wriggled out of my arms and made a beeline to where Cyn had opened a can of food and set it on the floor. I rolled to my feet and walked across the empty room to where he stood.

"If we were very lucky, your timely intervention blew

their alliance sky high." Cyn draped an arm around my shoulders. "What I suspect happened is Medusa and her sisters stepped in and told the men to stuff their bent-out-of-shape dicks up their asses."

The visual was hilarious, but I wasn't in a laughing mood. "What can you tell me about the Shadow Lords. Why are they even involved? Who freed them from the dragons' prison?"

"'Fraid I can't shed a whole lot of light on any of those questions," Cyn replied and pulled me closer against him. "Like many myths and legends, the ones about them have swirled, surfaced, and retreated. Because they weren't around for the last millennium or so, most of us—me included—assumed they were gone for good."

"But what were they like before they sank into oblivion?" I pressed, hungry for details. Anything would be better than what I had, which was pretty much nothing.

"You know how some creatures absorb goodness and innocence, reflecting it back?" Cyn tilted his head to meet my gaze. When I nodded, he continued. "The Shadow Lords thrive on evil, on chaos. They've been the force behind every mishap, every misfortune to befall all worlds."

"How is that possible if they haven't been around?"

"What I said was they dropped out of sight," Cyn

clarified. "Became the stuff of nightmares. While I knew the dragons had done something to confine them, I had no idea it was supposed to be permanent until their seers told us." He narrowed his eyes. "So many should haves. I should have asked more questions, should have looked for the Shadow Lords to satisfy myself they'd been neutralized. No excuses. I assumed Oberon had taken care of anything that needed to be done."

"He was taking care of it, all right," I muttered. "That may have been when he fell prey to whatever inducements they offered for his aid. I wasn't so much asking after their history, though. What powers their magic? How can they be hobbled?"

"Did Auril teach you about balance points? About light and dark energies and how they exist in a dynamic equilibrium?"

"Some," I said.

"The short version is the Shadow Lords are fallen kings—and queens. They choose evil and were banished from their respective lands. Over an exceedingly long time, they found one another. Not all at once, but in twos and threes. Recognizing they had common roots, they quested about for a way they could sow chaos. What they settled on was singling out a world, separating it from all others, and establishing themselves as rulers. Once they'd quelled any resistance, they lived on the magic inherent in that realm, redirecting it to their purposes."

"How many of them are there?" I asked.

He shrugged. "Hard to say. Something under ten, I'd guess. Perhaps fewer than six. The most I've ever seen in one spot is four."

"Seems manageable," I ventured. Done with his food, Midnight was winding in and out of my legs, purring like a mad thing.

"On their own, aye," Cyn agreed. "It's fortunate we didn't face them during your end run. They'd have increased Pegasus's inherent wickedness."

"And the Unseelie?"

"They're a mixed bag," Cyn replied. "They can be reasonable, but the King of Winter went off the deep end when Auril told him to piss up a rope."

"Are the Shadow Lords smarter than the Winter King and Pegasus?" Before Cyn answered, I went on, "I arrived prepared to fight my way out of there. They took one look at me, underestimated my skills, and didn't take any precautions at all."

"They're canny, shrewd, and older than you can imagine. You won't get to play the innocent card again," Cyn cautioned me. "The element of surprise only works once. I'm certain they tried to follow us—and failed."

"Probably so. We should get back to Faery, but first I need to tell you something."

He arched a brow. "What might it be?"

"Were you aware Danu is my grandmother?"

The shock on his face was answer enough before he sputtered, "How is that possible? She and Titania are sisters, and—"

"They had different mothers," I broke in. "The dragon seers told me. I rather innocently asked Mother if she could sweettalk her mother into helping us. After a spate of denials, she blew up and walked away.

"Titania made it clear Mother's parentage had to remain secret but didn't tell me why before she took off after Mother."

"The plot thickens," Cyn murmured. "Seems like Auril's relationship with Danu could be a strong drawing card."

"You'd think," I said. "No doubt we'll find out more as time goes on, but Mother's reaction surprised me." I stopped chewing my lower lip. "We shouldn't tarry much longer here, but I wanted to make certain you knew about Mother."

"I was just thinking the same thing." He nuzzled my neck. "Your spell or mine?"

"I'm easy. Go for it." Bending, I stroked Midnight and told him I'd try to come back soon, but not to worry if I didn't. Guess I was over my gloom-and-doom predictions where I'd taken pains to warn my feline companion I might never return. Nothing in my circumstances had changed, but tackling Pegasus and the Winter King dude had definitely improved my confidence. Especially after my dust-up with Mother.

I'd waltzed in—and out—of the Unseelie camp. Whacked a bee's nest in the process and lived to fight another day.

"Don't get too frisky." Cyn elbowed me.

"In my head again, were you?"

"It's quite instructive. Plus whatever the dragons' ritual did to us, it greased the skids for a quick peek."

I snorted. "Quick peek, my ass. You've taken up residence, but I can't think of anyone I'd rather have in my head." A second snort followed the first. "Once we get back and I fess up about what I did, you'll have plenty of company."

"I bet I will. Your mother will never let you out of her sight again." He grinned. It made him look young and carefree, but I wasn't fooled.

"Don't forget Titania. And Ysir is his own brand of powerhouse. He's so understated, it took me a while to sort things out, but he commands as much talent as Mother."

"Someone else said something like that," Cyn agreed. "Can't recall who right now, and it's probably not important."

The scents of his magic wafted through my flat. Whisky, wildflowers, and a musky mélange that made me wish we had more time. We emerged in dense woodland behind the Midnight Court's altar. Mother stood tall, a flowing ivory gown rustling in wind that only blew next to her. Her hair was unbound; warmth and compassion streamed from her. The glade was full of mages singing, loving, eating, and drinking. Animals had formed clusters around the revelers; birds flew overhead, even the ones who normally slept through the dark hours.

I'd never seen Mother's court, but Cyn's spell hadn't quite dissipated when a sense of rightness, wholeness, and peace descended on me. "This is quite amazing," I said near his ear.

"It is," he agreed. "Every time I dropped in, I swore I'd come more often, but other things always intervened. It didn't help that I caught grief from Oberon on the occasions he tracked me here."

Maybe her maternal instinct was working overtime, but Mother glided next to us. I dropped a shield over my mind, but it turned out I needn't have bothered. News travels fast in Faery, even to a place like the Midnight Court that's separated from the rest of the world by a magical veil.

"I should scold the living daylights out of you," she said in her low, raspy voice. "Instead, I'm proud you're my daughter. What you did was incredibly dangerous, and gutsy."

Interesting. She'd gotten over her bad mood from earlier. I turned to her. "You do understand why I didn't throw a public forum to hash through the issue. Decisions by committee rarely go well."

She nodded. "I do. It's much the same as when I decided to have you. I made my own choices and ran with them."

"Are Pegasus and your erstwhile consort still arguing?" Cyn spoke up.

"From what the birds are telling me, aye," Mother replied. "It makes our plans for tomorrow even more timely."

"It looks as if everyone is having a wonderful evening." I extended an arm toward the revelers. "When are you going to tell them?"

"I already have," she said. "Titania and Ysir and I did, but they deserve this small respite. Some of them, perhaps many, won't make it through tomorrow." She flapped her hands at Cyn and me. "Go. Dance. Forget about everything for a while. We will gather an hour before dawn to finalize our strike plans."

Cyn's arm was still around me, and he tugged me toward the glade. Nightingales sang, providing a sweet, haunting melody. I wanted everything. To dance and kick up my heels. To melt into Cyn's arms, but the dragons were still an unknown.

"I haven't heard from Ash," I told Mother. "Means I have to stop by Fire Mountain."

Auril wrapped her arms around me. "I will do that on your behalf, Daughter."

Before I could protest, she shimmered into motes of light.

"Whatever you want to do works for me," Cyn said. "If you want to draw diagrams for tomorrow, I'll sit with you and add my two cents."

"More like you doing that and me nattering on the sidelines," I said. "Remember? No actual soldier training."

He turned to me, his eyes serious. "You may not think you had any, but your mother spent all the years you were growing up honing you for the coming days."

Old irritations pushed to the fore but didn't burn as brightly as they once had. "I still think she should have told me more."

"Aye, but she didn't. Can't change the past. How about one dance? And then we'll find Ysir and work on what tomorrow is going to look like."

I'd caught glimpses of the ancient librarian—who appeared a few centuries younger than when I'd met him —twirling and stomping with a couple of fauns and faeries with dappled wings. It decided me. "All right," I told Cyn. Taking his hand, I walked by his side until we joined a group of satyrs and unicorns engaged in a variation of line dancing.

The nightingales' song swelled through me, filled me with delight and hope. Partway through the first dance, an imposing woman glided between Cyn and a satyr, taking his other hand. It required a shot of surreptitious magic before I recognized Faery had joined us.

## CHAPTER TWELVE, CYN

Surprise thrummed through me when Faery grabbed my other hand. Surprise and a jolt that intensified my ties with her. Burying my suspicions deep, I hoped she wouldn't pick up on them. No matter how benign she appeared, she'd released Oberon when she could have kicked him to the curb. Permanently.

Our last go-round hadn't gone well. She'd been angry, and I'd been bitter. Given the specter of tomorrow's battle looming over us all, the prudent course would be to pretend our argument never happened.

I could do that.

I'd expected her to be furious Dariyah and I were mated, but she hadn't said a word about it. Perhaps I wouldn't remind her of that, either. Although when the dragons showed up, the bond would become much more palpable. Faery never did anything without design. She hadn't dropped in on the Midnight Court to dance a few reels.

Oh hell no. She had something in mind. Either she'd intuited we marched into battle tomorrow—or someone had told her. Was she spying for the Unseelie? Would she carry our plans to their war camp? I tweaked my link with her, testing it. Because it was so new, I didn't understand how it worked. Was it a two-way street? If she lied, would I know?

To cover the small bit of expended magic she must have felt at her end, I said, "Lovely to see you."

She kicked up her heels as the line switched direction. "You have no idea how much I've missed being able to do things like this."

"Must have been difficult." I nodded and did my best to project empathy. May as well grab the bull by the horns, though. "Did you stop by Dubrova on your way here?"

A neutral inquiry. What would she do with it?

Faery tossed back her head; musical laughter rolled from her throat. "I did." Letting go of my hand, she muscled between Dariyah and me. "The horse and Unseelie king are still slugging it out. You're braver than I gave you credit for, child," she told Dariyah.

"Mother said much the same." Dariyah scowled. "Why'd everyone assume I was a coward?"

"Eh, there's courage and then there's going above and beyond. What would you have done if they'd captured you?" Faery missed a step or two because the whole of her attention was zeroed in on Dariyah.

"I'm tough to catch." Dariyah grinned. "Just ask Oberon. He tried and failed so many times, he gave up."

"Aye, but he's lazy," Faery retorted. "Makes a difference."

"Do you know about tomorrow?" I asked a second neutral question since Faery had answered the first in a way that didn't get my hackles up.

"Titania and Ysir alerted me," Faery said. "You might try doing the same."

I started to point out we'd nearly come to blows during my last visit to the cavern beneath Faery. Instead, I piled another question on top of the last one. "Do you have opinions about the wisdom of our strategy?"

"What do you think?" The old, imperious Faery was back in full bloom.

"Of course, you would," I murmured, still working on diplomacy. Her future was at stake right along with all the rest of ours. What I didn't know was if she'd hedged her bets by playing both ends against the middle.

The nightingales were winding down. I'd have liked nothing better than another dance, but duty beckoned.

Beckoned, eh? If our straits hadn't been so dire, I'd have laughed at my choice of concepts. I was fooling myself and sunk in denial if I visualized duty crooking fingers my way as if maybe I had a choice.

I had to trust Faery at this point. Titania and Ysir did, and neither was the gullible sort. But they hadn't gotten into a spat with her, either. Our dancing partners drifted away, perhaps sensing discord between Faery and her regent. Or maybe I was reading too much into it.

Faery still stood on my left with Dariyah on my other side. I turned so I faced her. "Apologies for the earlier unpleasantness between us."

"Accepted."

Dariyah glided off to one side and sent a pointed glance my way over Faery's shoulder, clearly in favor of Faery offering her own apology. It would never happen; besides, it was only words. "Will you be present tomorrow?" I asked.

Faery bristled. "Why wouldn't I be?"

I raised a conciliatory hand. "Not what I meant. We will be solidifying our offensive. Your presence will strengthen our efforts."

"Good you recognize it," Faery fired back.

Dariyah hooked a hand through my bent arm. "When Medusa shanghaied me, you hung me out to dry telling me I'd figure things out. Turns out I did, but not without a few quick changes. Tomorrow we will fight for your integrity, your existence. If Mother is correct, and she almost always is, what happens tomorrow will not be definitive. Still, winning can only help us over the long haul. What Cyn is asking is what role you will assume. Are you planning to lead troops? Will you add magic from the sidelines?"

"Why must I choose now?" Faery straightened her back. "I will add my efforts where they are needed most."

"If everyone did that," I told her, "we would lose. Warcraft requires a coordinated approach with everyone in their assigned roles. You may select any position, any role, you wish, but no matter how things are going, you will need to stick with it if you're visible and on the front lines."

"If no one knows you're there"—Dariyah continued my line of thought—"you'll have a lot more latitude. A landslide here, an earthquake there. Maybe a rift or two that conveniently swallows a whole platoon of Unseelie."

"If you struck where no one could anticipate your moves, it would be extremely useful," I tossed out.

"I will consider your opinion," Faery said. "When will decisions be finalized?"

I couldn't not tell her. The simple fact of my hesitation screamed I wasn't certain of her intentions, didn't totally trust her. To cover my ambivalence, I glanced Dariyah's way. "What did your mother say about that?"

"Return here before dawn," she said.

Faery drew her cloak more snugly around her and vanished without a word.

A breathy sigh rattled from Dariyah. "That one requires kid gloves. Did I say something wrong?"

"Probably the 'return here' part sounded a lot like an order. In her world, she isn't on the receiving end of them. But the one who stepped in shit was me. The pause when she asked about our pre-battle meeting wasn't wise."

"I didn't notice one."

"Aye, but I'm certain she did. I might not know Faery all that intimately, but she's made it her business to know about me and every other mage who's held any kind of power position on her world. Besides, she reads my thoughts through her link with me. I slathered spells over the worst of my misgivings, but I'm not certain she didn't drill right through them."

"Nothing you can do about it now. She will either show up and fight alongside us. Or she'll sit this one out kind of like when she left me to my fate dangling from Medusa's claws."

I drew Dariyah into my arms, threading my fingers into her silky wing feathers. "You've mentioned it more than a few times. Is it still bothering you?"

She made a small shrugging movement. "Not really. It wasn't so much that she left, but the way she did so.

She wasn't honest. Drummed up some crap about her world needing her, but when she returned here she didn't do much of anything to help those fighting for her. She wasn't present to assist with healing the wounded, either."

Moving a hand from her wings to her head, I smoothed stray locks of hair away from her face. "Faery isn't easy to trust, but perhaps it's more us than her. She operates on a completely different wavelength. What I'm worried might be treachery could be just who she is."

Dariyah's green gaze bored into me. "Nice save, but I don't buy it. No matter whose rules you play by, prioritizing your own hide doesn't play well."

"We won't change her," I pointed out.

"I get that. And wishing she were different probably pisses her off and makes her think we don't appreciate her." Dariyah shook her head. "Not a problem we're going to solve."

"True enough, and she was probably listening to every word."

"I disagree," Dariyah said. "In her worldview, we're not important enough to bother with."

A small ensemble of satyrs had begun to play instruments that looked like oversized fiddles. "Feel like another dance?" I asked. "Or would you rather work on tomorrow?"

"It's today, actually. Midnight's come and gone."

I held her tighter against me, reveling in the feel of her body molded to mine. Between us, my cock thickened and pressed into her belly. I knew how I wanted to spend the next bit of time. Rising on tiptoe, Dariyah brushed her lips across mine. The touch of them was exquisite, light as butterfly wings. She wrapped her arms around me, strong fingers stroking my back and sending erotic streams of wonder through my body.

And then, her wings spread and folded around both of us. Otherworldly sensations buffeted me. I'd never been encased in wings before. They were warm, tingly, alive with her essence, her heat, her scent.

Her tongue was in my mouth, questing and probing. Where her breasts were smushed against my chest, the nipples formed hard peaks. The satyrs' music, full of sensual urging, filled the glade. All around us, the sounds of passion blossomed, and I remembered earlier trysts in this same glade.

Satyrs bleed lust; it's their métier. Smothered in wings and Dariyah, I didn't glance about, but if I had I was certain I'd find Pan leading his horny crew as they played and stroked engorged members. The hotter they got, the randier their song.

Dariyah snaked a hand between us and curved her fingers around my achingly hard cock. Soon, she'd made short work of my zipper, and I melted into skin-to-skin contact. Courtesy of the Midnight Court and Dariyah's charms, I'd gone from mild arousal to harder-than-hard in moments. Dropping my hands to her waist, I grappled with the fastenings of her pants. Once I got them unzipped, I pushed a hand between her legs, delighting in the slick heat coating my fingers.

She broke our kiss long enough to pant, "I miss skirts."

"They were simpler," I agreed and moved one hand to cradle the side of her face as I reveled in her beauty, in the rose splotches of passion dappling her face. A full moon hung over the glade, providing plenty of illumination. At least in this corner of Faery, the moon was always full. The satyrs had begun to sing along with their instruments. The song, in ancient Gaelic, urged revelry, lust, unbridled restraint. The nightingales, who'd been silent for a while, added their throaty melody to the mix.

"I don't want to let go," Dariyah said as she untangled wings and arms and fingers. Bending, she unlaced her boots and toed them off. It freed a path for me to push her pants down her legs. Once she'd stepped out of them, she held up her arms, spread her wings wide, and said, "Lift me."

Threading my arms around her, I took the firm globes of her amazing ass in my hands and got a solid grip. Forearms sliding along her thighs, I raised her until she wrapped her legs around my waist and her arms around my shoulders. For long, tantalizing moments, I balanced her so the tip of my cock sat squarely at the entrance to her body.

And then I lowered her onto my shaft as slowly as I could manage. Sparks flew, igniting into an inferno, as she stretched to accommodate me. Time stopped, swirling around us, until I was fully encased in the miracle of her body. Where her wings had been spread, she'd brought them close, circling us in their silvery fluff.

She sank her teeth into my shoulder and raked nails down my back. "Move, goddammit."

I crushed my mouth over hers, biting her full lower lip as I withdrew almost as slowly as I'd entered. More strokes, breathtakingly slow, incredibly erotic. She rocked her torso against me, brushing the tips of her nipples back and forth against my chest. I wanted to roll them, enhance her arousal, except we were pretty white-hot in that department as it was.

Shrieks and moans escalated around us as other couplings reached the point of ecstasy once or many times. Without realizing it was happening, we'd picked up the pace. No longer slow, we fucked with abandon, almost as if the glade held its own agenda not only for us, but for everyone ranged around it.

I felt Dariyah's orgasm before it rushed through her, but I hung onto my own. I cheated. Without magic, I'd have come right along with her. Between the musk of our combined arousal, the satyrs' song, and the power of hundreds of mages all having sex in one iteration or another, the drive for release was overpowering.

Her vault contracted around me as her next peak seeded itself from the one that had just rolled through her. She grabbed my head, fingers tangled in my hair. Before she covered my mouth with her own, she said, "Now. With me."

My balls snugged against my body, but still I waited until her muscles tightened around me, vibrating with release. Semen gushed in a burning flood of satisfaction. My arms and legs shook as I gave myself up to one of the oldest magics of them all.

We strained against one another as our passion played itself out. Still encased in her body, I found enough breath to tell her I loved her.

"The feeling is mutual," she murmured.

I lifted her off my still stiff cock and held her tight against me. The placement of her wings shifted in the process and shrouded me in downy feathers. "They're a nice touch," I said.

She laughed softly. "They seem to be. I was worried they'd get in the way, but they didn't. Let go. I need my clothes."

I could have held her forever, but the glade was emptying out. At some point, the music had died away, and the satyrs were gone. If Pan had really been here, I hadn't seen him. But you have to be quick to catch a glimpse of that one. He's always been elusive with his flute and flagon of spirits.

I cleaned myself with soft handfuls of grass; Dariyah did the same. She had more to do with dressing than me, but she put herself back to rights quickly. When she looked up, a soft smile graced her features. "Now we can get to some serious planning."

"We were going to do that before," I reminded her.

"Who knows? Maybe what we did will be essential to victory? Mother always taught me not to question strong magic, to run with it and see where it led."

Deep laughter alerted me Auril was near. "Never thought I'd live long enough to hear you quote me."

"Don't spread it around," Dariyah joked back, "but I've often repeated things you said."

"I won't let it go to my head." Auril was still laughing. "Come on. Playtime is over. We have work to do."

"Did you..." Dariyah hesitated before adding, "take advantage of tonight's court?"

"Why, Daughter, what a personal question. Since you asked, Pan is an old friend. He doesn't visit often, but when he does, his power is impossible to resist."

"Will he help us fight?" I asked.

Auril's laughter had shaded to chuckles. "Oh my, no. He's a lover that one, not a fighter, but his actions tonight will strengthen the satyrs and all the rest of us too." She blew out a breath. "Everything slots together in the magical world. Never forget that part. Even the most insignificant details, items you're certain are meaningless, often swim to the surface. And then you remember something important, something that wouldn't have registered if you hadn't been paying attention."

"There you go, back into riddle mode," Dariyah murmured.

"No riddles there, Daughter. What I said is never underestimate anything."

"Thank you for tonight." I inclined my head Auril's way.

"None needed. Dariyah was correct. Tonight had to unfold precisely as it did. Sex holds power, and it will bolster our warriors for the morrow. When the battle turns against us—and it will—the added sweetness of memories may be the lynchpin that pulls us through."

So long as she was in a sharing mood, I lowered my voice and asked, "What role will the land play?"

Auril drew her russet brows together. "Funny you should ask that. I've been trying to scry an answer to the same question for a few days now and coming up emptyhanded."

"Guess it will be a surprise," Dariyah mumbled.

"Aye, for all of us," I said.

"Have faith." Auril's tone was sharp. "This is her bailiwick. No one loses worse than her if we fail."

*Unless she's signed on with the other side.*

I buried the thought deep, not allowing it to do more than tiptoe across the surface of my mind. Guess I didn't do as well at stealth as I thought because Auril gripped my arm and said, "We'll find out soon enough. Come on. The others are waiting for us."

"The dragons," Dariyah asked. "Are they coming?"

"Of course. They're part of the history that will unfold soon, and they know as much."

"Did you go to Fire Mountain?" I inquired.

She nodded. "Aye, but they were readying themselves to leave anyway. The magical world is joined in ways I've been sorting for a long while."

We trudged to the far side of the green, each lost in our own thoughts. Mine strayed to the passion Dariyah and I had shared. I didn't push the imagery away. Battle would be upon us soon, obliterating everything pleasant.

"We'll come through this," Dariyah said.

I took her hand, not as certain we'd prevail as she was. *Believing is half the battle,* I reminded myself. Everything magical begins with visualizing the endpoint.

"Magic 101," Auril said crisply.

I might have felt chagrined my musings were on display—if I hadn't been so concerned about protecting

Faery's people. War leaves scars on the living, deep ones that last forever.

Redirecting my misgivings into action, I focused on tomorrow. On how we'd come out slugging and make it so miserable for the Unseelie they'd tell their king to go fuck himself.

## CHAPTER THIRTEEN, DARIYAH

I hadn't been especially nervous before, and I wasn't exactly apprehensive now, but my spine crawled with pins and needles. Even my wings didn't feel as comforting as they had since they'd sprouted. Faery had shown up for our final planning session midway through. Despite being late, she'd been reasonably appropriate. She hadn't said much, though, and I still wasn't certain what she was going to do. Frankly, I hoped she opted for creating chaos from the sidelines.

Dragons were still drifting in. Mages from places I'd never heard of accompanied them. I assumed they were part of the Elderkin network. Skinwalkers, ghosts, sprites, gnomes, and dwarves.

"That's all of us," Ash rumbled from where he stood a few feet away.

The entire glade was full of mages. Ysir and the dragons and unicorns had split the mass into fighting groups, building on work Ysir had been doing with them. I had no idea what the Elderkin mages could do, but the dragons did. We tried for a complementary mix of magics in each faction.

Despite everyone in Faery who was capable of fighting showing up, we'd still be badly outnumbered. Cyn had asked Faery pointblank if any new fissures had formed, places the Unseelie might augment their ranks. She'd said no. I wished I had more faith in her answer.

Any propensity I might have had to trust her had taken a powder when she'd left me to Medusa's not-so-tender mercies. I really needed to let it go. Every time I thought of Faery, I was right back dangling from Medusa's bony fingers, smelling the poison from vipers circling her head, and cringing at their discordant hissing.

If the situation rose again, Faery would desert me just as fast. It shouldn't bother me. It wasn't as if I'd spent my life waiting around to be rescued. Nope. Always did my own scut work in that regard. Actually, her rapid egress had done me two favors: forced me to rely on my own resources and dodged the problem of her not wanting to cede my body back to me.

I may have dunned myself for feeling raw and used by Faery, but this latest twist snapped me out of my funk. She truly had done me a favor. If we ever chatted again, I'd make a point of sweetly thanking her. Ha. That should get her good. In her heart of hearts—if she even possessed such a thing—she probably assumed she was leaving me to die. Her pep talk about being certain I'd find a way out was to salve her own guilt.

Cyn headed up one of the groups. I was in another with Ash, several unicorns, and five other dragons. They'd assigned me to this group because we'd tag-team our efforts between air and land. Presumably, we'd face others with flight capacity—the Gorgons and Pegasus and perhaps Chrysaor depending on which form he selected. Two other dragon-heavy groups would be working with us.

Hawks would do double duty, both fighting and providing communication between groups that didn't rely on telepathy, which could be intercepted. The sky was developing gray edges along the horizon. I'd been waiting for evidence dawn was upon us, and dreading it both.

Time to leave.

Cyn ran lightly to me and swept me into a quick, hard hug. "Don't take any chances," he murmured, following it with, "Never mind. You'll fight and fight well. Come back to me in one piece."

I leaned into him before letting go. "I'll tell you the

same thing. Our fates are linked. I felt it happen after the dragons' ritualistic ceremony."

"Aye, 'twill make keeping tabs on you easier." He grinned, boyish and engaging, but it was a front. Engaging, yeah, but nothing boyish about my thousand-year-old mate.

Mother, Ysir, and Titania joined us. Each headed groups of mixed mages. "Ready?" Mother's brisk tone was all business, but I knew her well, and she wasn't as sanguine as she appeared. Storm clouds had gathered; she'd been waiting for this moment ever since she decided to follow her visions and create me. But only a fool runs headlong into war, and Mother was far from stupid.

"Aye, let's get moving." Cyn locked gazes with Ysir. "No heroics. Keep our casualty count down."

The old seer nodded in understanding. "We'll do our best. Everyone recognizes the stakes. If the tide turns against us, though..."

He didn't finish his thought, but I knew what he'd left out. Losing would place us in an untenable position, worse than the last time we'd lost. If things didn't go our way, Faery's ground would run red with blood, and not just that of our enemies. I wished I knew more about what plans Faery had—or if she was even completely loyal to our cause. She'd displayed as much of her hand as she wanted to. Cyn had poked and prodded, angling for more details, and gotten nowhere.

In my limited experience, Faery was rarely forthright. This had to be one more example of the land simply being herself. I refused to entertain the possibility she was lurking on the sidelines and would throw her lot in with whomever appeared to be winning. If that was her plan, it would piss me off so much, I'd probably storm her cave and confront her.

An unbelievably bad idea on the leading edge of today.

The next part fuzzed out. I don't exactly remember flying to the rest of my group, but the dragons and I had a journey casting at the ready. When it faded, we stood on a knoll about half a mile from what was left of Dubrova. Our assigned hawks flew to let the other groups know we were in position. Birds were ubiquitous in Faery, and there was no way for the Unseelie to determine this batch was working on our side.

We waited until the birds returned to confirm everyone was in place. The plan was a coordinated attack from every side. At least so far, the Unseelie appeared unaware we were about to bear down on them. I still didn't know jack about the Shadow Lords, but I'd find out quick enough once one showed up. Anything magical can be defused, but some magic-wielders require a whole lot more effort than others.

Adrenaline coursed through me. My wings quivered with anticipation. Ash leapt skyward, golden wings spread wide. It was the signal I'd been waiting for; our group was on the move. I cleared my mind of everything —and everyone. Of Cynwrigg and Mother, the two people I loved in this world. Of Faery's incredible mages, many of whom wouldn't live to see the newly risen sun set later today.

I launched after the third dragon, and we flew in formation with me in the middle of six of them. Part of me chafed at them protecting me, while another wiser part recognized I lacked scales. Dragons were nearly impossible to kill. Nothing penetrated their hides, whereas I was far more fragile. I'd expected maybe something like the mithril vests from *Lord of the Rings*, but no one in Faery bothered with armor, viewing it as the purview of mortals. The other dragon groups met us in the air. Unicorns and a variety of other mages ran beneath our flight path rousting out whatever crossed their route.

As we grew closer to the Unseelie encampment, shouts and cries suggested they'd figured out they were under attack. Warriors piled out of tents, sloppy gouts of power spiraling outward as they employed the scatter approach assuming if they tossed enough magic about they'd hit something.

The dragons flying with me spewed fire with laser-like precision, incinerating whatever they aimed at. Destructive magic bounced between my outstretched hands. So far, I hadn't found anything to chuck it at. The dragons were doing a bang-up job of clearing Unseelie, the mages beneath us chivvied into the open.

A hawk flew close, dipping and weaving and squawking. Ash altered our trajectory a few degrees eastward. Below us, columns of mages clashed against one another. The Unseelie had gotten themselves organized. Unicorns gored them, but a seemingly endless supply of uninjured warriors rolled forward. Because of my aerial vantage point, the mismatch in our numbers was obvious—and staggering.

Even if none of the Gorgons showed up, we were bound to lose, mowed under by the sheer mass of our enemy. Working in efficient lines, the dragons painted the ground with fire. Much like magefire, dragonfire burns with a life all its own. It can't be doused with water. I hadn't realized that part until a few Unseelie threw themselves into the moat.

So far, I'd been dead weight. My palms tingled from holding onto lethal power for far too long. Selecting a small circle of Unseelie who were intent on trapping a unicorn, I loosed my magic, spreading it to encompass half the circle. At least it would provide an escape route for the trapped unicorn. His horn was dappled with crimson, and he reared and pawed the ground.

My aim was true, but then it always had been. The only difference was I was firing from the air not the ground. Five Unseelie fell to their knees, clutching their chests. They'd recover, but it would take a while. The unicorn didn't wait for a second invitation. He launched himself over their sprawled bodies and cantered to a safer spot, joining another of our factions.

I directed additional power into a second volley, so I'd be ready to go again. The stench of burning flesh and spilled entrails rose to meet us. Bushes and trees smoldered from dragonfire that had spilled beyond its targets. I craned my neck, working to increase my angle of vision beyond the bulk of all the dragons surrounding me.

Where was Cyn?

For that fact, was Faery doing anything to help us? If she'd created any natural disasters like slides or rockfall, it hadn't been obvious from where I flew. Maybe my speculation she was waiting to see who appeared to be winning hadn't been far off the mark.

I forced my mind away from possible treachery, reminded myself she'd saved me after I'd healed the rift cleaving her in two. She could just as easily have left me an empty husk, but she didn't. Beneath me, four satyrs surrounded one of their own who'd fallen. The dragon next to me picked off a group of Unseelie headed their way.

The dragons appeared to be enjoying themselves as they filled the air with smoke and ash. But then, they trained to be warriors almost from the day they hatched. I liked the flying part, but the battle on the ground was unnerving. I started to reach for Cyn with my mind voice, but didn't. What if I diverted him at a critical moment? One where if he'd had access to his full attention, he'd have prevailed.

He was still on his feet, still fighting. I'd know if he'd fallen. For now, it would have to be enough.

"There they are," Ash trumpeted and banked hard left.

Nothing had changed on the ground. Who was he referring to? And then I saw the problem. My heartbeat quickened; breath caught in my throat. Medusa and another of the Gorgons winged toward us, flying almost lazily, as if they weren't the least bit concerned. The reek of poison, a stench that was stenciled into my nose from my last go-round with her, wafted toward me in thick billowy waves.

Power sheeted around the monsters, bombarding us like turbulence from a jet taking off. My wings cleaved the air, seeking purchase, but it was spotty. The dragons' wings were far larger than mine; they did better remaining airborne. Despite my best efforts, I dropped at least fifty feet and fought to remain upright. Blasts of power threatened to tip me onto my back.

A swooshing from behind me sent ice chips scuttling down my spine. Was this when I fell out of the sky? I twisted myself into a pretzel and saw Ash a moment before his comforting bulk slid beneath me. Settling onto his back, I folded my wings. "Thanks."

He wasn't paying me the slightest attention, though. Fire streamed from his open jaws, aimed for Medusa and her sister. Apparently snakes were *de rigeur* for Gorgons since they all sported heads wreathed by vipers. I let power fly from my hands, directing all of it at Medusa. I may as well have inundated her with water for all the effect it had. If she noticed my supposedly lethal volley, it wasn't apparent.

Alrighty, then. I needed a plan B. When Ash got slightly closer, the better to inundate her with fire, I shouted, "How's it going, Granny?"

My magic hadn't gotten her attention, but my words did. She angled her whirling gaze, the one that turned mortals to stone, my way and leered. "You might come in useful, girlie."

I bristled and unfurled my wings, ready to trade Ash's back for hers. *"Stay put,"* the dragon's deep voice rushed through my mind. My bond to dragonkind thrummed. Had he done something to ensure I remained on his back? I'd have carped at him except he was fully engaged in an aerial firefight. Well, fire on his side, poison from the other.

Where they met in the air between us, they sizzled ominously. The poison seemed to feed the fire, forcing flames hundreds of feet into the air. The smoke, already thick and noxious, grew a hundred times worse. Dragons have an extra clear eyelid. I don't. Seeing grew progressively more difficult, so I switched to my psychic view.

Ash and a blue dragon focused their fire on Medusa and her sister; the others continued to aid our ground effort. At least two unicorns had fallen; the loss made my heart hurt. I wasn't doing enough up here. If I had boots on the ground, I could get down and dirty, fighting the way I was used to. One enemy at a time.

Could I leave if I wanted to, or had Ash tethered me to him? He was trying to keep me safe, but I hadn't done too badly in that department.

"Give us the woman," Medusa snarled.

"Aye, if you hand her over, we will direct the Unseelie to retreat." The other Gorgon smiled, displaying rows of rotting teeth.

"Never," Ash shot back.

"She is an abomination," Medusa went on. "Formed from treachery, her very existence bodes ill for everyone."

"Pot. Kettle," I called across the air separating us. "Or maybe it takes one to know one."

The air around her hazed red as anger streamed from her, mingling with jets of poison from her pet snakes.

One of them jumped the gap, no doubt with a magical assist, and landed on my thigh. I killed it with a thought before it could sink its fangs into me.

As it writhed in death throes, I shot magic through it, hunting for a way to neutralize its kin winding around the Gorgons' heads. The snake was only partially "real." Much of it had been shaped with dark magic. Anything created with enchantment can be uncreated the same way.

A hasty assessment of the scaled body suggested it was mostly fire with a small amount of air, which meant water and earth could defeat it. I wanted to let Ash, who was still banking and weaving and feinting to avoid any more viper passengers, know what I was up to. Even stray thoughts from me could be intercepted, though, so I quietly ginned up what I hoped would annihilate the rest of the serpents.

Next to me, a red dragon winked out of existence. One minute he was flying, the next he wasn't there. Crap. What had happened?

"No more snakes," Ash thundered.

"But they're so useful," Medusa purred. "Why, one of my darlings found her way beneath that dragon's scales. With predictable results."

At least it explained the red dragon's hasty egress. I bet he was beating a path back to Fire Mountain and the dragon healers. My casting was nearly ready. No reason to hold back. I didn't need perfection, only something that worked. I started with the other Gorgon with her porcelain skin and wispy violet hair. Like Medusa, she wore a silken robe wrapped around her body with large holes to accommodate her wings.

One power word blasted from me, followed by two more.

"What are you about?" Ash asked sharply.

All I told him was, "Wait."

This would work. Or it wouldn't. If not, I'd alter my proportions of elements. Regardless, something would happen, and it would be instructive for my next go at the problem.

The Gorgon grabbed her head, shouting, "Not me, you idiots."

I felt like cheering. My magic hurt the vipers. Because snakes aren't all that smart to begin with, they'd assumed the pain arose from their mistress and acted in kind by biting her.

I didn't expect their venom to be toxic to her, but it could make her miserable. An image of the skin on Mother's foot sloughing off after one of Medusa's vipers had bitten her formed, and I smiled grimly.

Having the Gorgon's skin peel off her body was too much to hope for, but I'd take whatever damage the snakes dished out.

"What did you do?" Medusa shrieked and turned her attention toward her sister.

Rather than answering, I spewed more power words and repeated my actions except this time, they were aimed at Granny's head of writhing serpents.

"Nice work," Ash said quietly.

"Can you finish them off while they're busy?" I asked.

"Nay, but I can set their wings afire. They've been protecting them with magic." Ash sent a firestorm at Medusa's wings. The blue dragon we'd been working with did the same for the other Gorgon. Shrieking curses, they tumbled from the skies, wings ablaze and snakes scattering every which way.

I felt like cheering. Instead, I said, "I want to fight from the ground. It's what I know. What I'm used to."

"Cyn made me promise to keep you safe," Ash replied. "I can do that up here, not so much below."

"Who's keeping him safe?" I countered, suddenly desperate to lay eyes on him and reassure myself he was still whole. If I trusted our shared magic he was, but there's no substitute for confirmation.

The swoosh of wings drew my eyes upward. Had Medusa and her sister recovered so quickly? I didn't see how they could have. But it wasn't them. Pegasus's great wings sliced through the air as he flew right toward us. Ash fanned his wings, positioning us to fight back.

I readied magic, waiting for the atrocity who was my

father to come close enough for me to inflict maximum damage. I'd maintained a ward through everything, so I wasn't expecting to be yanked off Ash's back into a casting that stank of the winged horse.

I summoned power like a mad thing, trying every neutralizing spell I knew to cut through Pegasus's enchantment before it dragged me goddess only knew where. Whatever spell I was trapped in had very little air. Between thrashing around trying to free myself and shuffling through counterspells, my chest grew tight, and my mind felt dull.

"You bested Mother," Pegasus neighed. "For that, I might spare your life."

"Let me go," I wheezed, clawing at my throat.

"Far too late for that. I do not care for surprises... Daughter. But I have one in store for you."

Before I could reply, my whirling head grew thicker still, and I plummeted into blackness, the battlefield disappeared quickly as we moved...elsewhere.

## 14

## CHAPTER FOURTEEN, CYN

The battle raged around me. My face stung
from a place some crafty Unseelie had
punched through my warding and scribed a
gash across my cheekbone. Obviously, I've fought
before, but the last really big battle was when the
dragons sealed the Shadow Lords into a supposedly
escape-proof container. There've been plenty of skirmishes in the intervening centuries, but nothing to rival
today.

Despite my best efforts, three of my company were
dead. Two satyrs and a unicorn. Their loss was intolera-
ble, but the Unseelie didn't care who they mowed
through. Apparently, their instructions were to spare no
one. I'd parleyed for the unicorn's life until he told me
not to grovel on his behalf. When the satyrs fell beneath

Unseelie blades, swords imbued with magic strong enough to end immortal lives, I got even and killed half a dozen.

Anger has always been a key element in my magic, strengthening it beyond my expectations. With my blade dialed to maximum lethal output, I cleaved through necks as fury carved a path through me. The infusion of dragon enchantment and my bond with both them and Dariyah added power to my efforts.

What had we come to? We were killing each other. I knew almost all the Unseelie who chopped through my company of mages. It made things worse to recall raising a pint or playing games of chance with a mage I'd just split in two. The ground ran slick with blood, so much blood I slipped and slid if I wasn't careful.

To keep my spirits up, I cursed Oberon roundly. If it weren't for him and his stupid, ill-advised dislike for everyone who wasn't Fae, we wouldn't be here. Or maybe I was wrong about that. Auril's foresights, her prophecies, weren't based on Oberon but on believing what the spirits or gods or whoever fueled her visions, had to say about the future.

Maybe she'd have seduced Pegasus even if Oberon had been a model liege. It seemed unlikely. Events dovetailed together, feeding off one another. What Auril scryed in her pool was someone's best guess about how the future would unfold given current events. Keeping my mind busy was my best hedge against letting pity stay my hand—or horror because I was killing someone I'd once broken bread with.

Random thoughts rolled this way and that as my blade rose and fell and rose again. Augmented with magic, my aim was always true. The stench of battle surrounded me. Sweat and blood and spilled entrails. War has a particular mélange of smells, none of them nice. I'd begun with 232 mages and an assortment of hawks. From time to time, a hawk landed on my shoulder and chittered while delivering messages about the other groups.

They were holding their own, but the flood of Unseelie hadn't slowed one whit. We'd helped our cause by shutting the portal to the world Titania had been held prisoner, but not by a whole lot. Where had all these Unseelie come from? When they'd left Faery, their numbers hadn't looked anything like this.

Blood dripped from my blade, running onto my hands. I hefted it and separated one more head from its associated body. A cursory glance at the head made me look again. Unless I was mistaken, this was Timmons, an Unseelie I'd already killed. Too late to ask him questions. The dead don't answer readily.

I drew a binding spell and snared the next Unseelie in line, another man I knew vaguely. "What's going on?" I demanded as fighting raged around me. Faery could have helped, but despite her encouraging words before dawn, I hadn't seen any evidence she was doing aught but sitting on the sidelines waiting.

The question was for what?

The Unseelie struggled against cords I'd bound him with and shrugged.

"Answer me, Shade," I growled.

"Or what? You're going to kill me, anyway." His pale gray eyes reflected bitter acceptance. He hadn't expected to walk out of Faery unscathed. What in the hell had the King of Winter done to his subjects? They'd always fought for him, but never been especially willing to lay down their lives on his behalf.

"Depends on your answer." I took a measured breath. "Not too late to switch sides."

"For me, it is."

I tightened the weave of my cage, making certain one of the bands pressed on his windpipe. "It appears I killed Timmons twice. How could that be?"

He raised weary eyes to mine. "They cloned us. How in the fuck else could we be so many?"

If I weren't so busy holding my enchantment in place, I'd have taken a few steps back. "Cloned you? How? Didn't you mind there'd be more than one of you?"

"Of course," he snarled with the first show of spirit

I'd seen. "You think we had a choice with Shadow Lords and Gorgons breathing down our necks?"

"How do you keep track of which of you was..." I floundered about at a loss for words.

"The original?" Shade supplied with a grimace.

"Something like that."

"We don't. We were told it didn't matter."

Because I wasn't paying close attention, a troll landed on my back and drove me into the dirt. It would play hell with the spell I'd bound Shade with, but I pulled magic like a madman, redirecting some of my power into defending myself. Trolls are made of stone, and they lack any magic at all. Normally, sunlight turns them immobile, but this one wasn't having any trouble beating his fists into my ribs and my head. I heard ribs breaking. Pain jabbed my sides; breathing grew more difficult.

Fuck! I hadn't come this far to have a piece of granite end me. Summoning a blast of air, I focused it right at the monster sprawled across my back. All of a sudden, the dead weight wasn't there any longer. My magic couldn't have worked that fast, but I'd take any help that fell my way. Not questioning my sudden good fortune, I rolled sideways and leapt to my feet pouring power into my broken places to speed their healing.

One of the unicorns had gored the troll right through an eye, the only part that wasn't solid rock.

Power flowed from Shade's upraised hands as he chanted softly. His casting washed against the troll's body just before it cracked into multiple pieces.

"Thanks," I muttered. "That offer about switching sides, it's—"

He waved me to silence. "No matter what I do at this point, they'll kill me, but I always respected you, Cynwrigg."

Before I could say anything more, he walked away. Perhaps he expected me to knife him in the back, but I don't roll that way. My group was holding their own. I left two unicorns in charge and set off in search of Ysir and Auril. There had to be some method of identifying the cloned Unseelies and neutralizing them. If we pared the enemy numbers down, we'd have a far better chance.

A hawk led me to Auril. I drew her off to one side and didn't mince words. "All those bazillions of Unseelie? They're clones."

"What? How'd you come to that conclusion?"

"Because I killed one twice. Remember, I know most of our enemy. When I jacked one up about what was going on, surprisingly, he came clean."

Auril narrowed her silver eyes. "Means their loyalty to their king isn't ironclad. We should be able to bend that to our advantage, and—"

"What we need to do," I spoke over her, "is determine how to disable the cloned versions."

"Absent knowing how they were created in the first place, it won't be easy."

"Nothing worthwhile ever is." I threw her own words back at her, unsure if she was who'd carped about that or someone else.

"I'll check in with Ysir," she said curtly. "We might come up with something effective between the two of us."

"Let me know if you require resources." I turned my next words toward the land as I hurried back to my company. *"Now would be a grand time to help us,"* I told Faery. The Unseelie king probably heard and was laughing his head off. I hadn't seen him—or the Shadow Lords. Were they having tea with Faery while waiting for us to fall under Unseelie heels?

For that fact, I hadn't seen the Gorgons, either. Or Pegasus. I draped myself in invisibility to speed my way. I'd never have left my troops if it hadn't been critical. I could have accomplished much the same with the hawk messengers, but it would have taken far longer.

My link to Dariyah snapped shut. What the hell? Had I tossed so much magic around I'd altered something? Cycling through channels I fully expected to sense her again, but she wasn't there. The dragons, yes. Dariyah, no.

My stomach twisted into a hard knot. My face and sides ached, but everything was minor compared with finding my mate, my love. I was torn. My troops needed me, but I had to search out what had happened to Dariyah. Faery stepped through a gash in the air. It might have been an act, but she had the grace to look worried.

"Dariyah is gone—" she began.

"I know." I cut her off. "Where is she?"

"Pegasus took her."

"You don't like her," I said pointblank. "Why are you telling me?"

"I may not like her, but her mother is part of me. Danu is Dariyah's grandmother. You must go after Dariyah, return her to her rightful home."

Apparently, everyone except me knew who Auril's mother was. I exhaled tiredly. "You mean the home Dariyah was deprived of most of her life?"

Faery shoved her face in front of mine. "I did not make the ridiculous rules about who could live here and who couldn't. Blame Oberon for that tripe." She snapped her fingers. "You're wasting time."

A shadow formed overhead. A big one. Ash thudded heavily to the ground next to us. "Come with me," he rumbled.

I didn't trust Faery as far as I could see her, but I did trust the dragon and leapt atop him. "We're tracking Dariyah," I said. It wasn't a question.

"Aye, but we have to hurry. It took me time to find

you, precious moments when we may have lost her trail entirely."

"Help Auril and Ysir. Take over leading my company, or find someone who can," I shouted at Faery and cut the flow of words. Dunning her for her seeming inactivity and lack of aid would only piss her off. She knew precisely what she'd done—and hadn't. Me spewing disappointment wouldn't move her off the dime.

Faery fell away as Ash's teleport spell ignited. I listened while he told me how they'd injured Medusa and her sister and how the horse had shown up out of nowhere and grabbed Dariyah. He'd carved through her warding as if it weren't there, which made some level of sense since they shared the same type of power.

But where had he taken her, and for what reason?

Rather than wasting time in speculation, I sent tracking magic in a wide arc. Complement to Ash's, we scoured every nook and cranny. "I can't find anything," I said after a few minutes.

"Me, either, but we have to keep trying," the dragon rumbled around clouds of smoke. "Since there's no trail to follow, we'll begin turning rocks over."

"If you mean we're going to move from place to place hunting them, it could take years," I protested.

The gold-scaled beast twisted his head until he looked right at me with his spinning eyes. "Do you have a better idea...Regent?"

The hesitation before my title spoke volumes, none of them good.

"Maybe if there were more of us—" I began.

"How? Everyone is engaged fighting." He flipped his head back to facing front.

I started to mention there had to be more dragons, ones who'd remained on Fire Mountain, but the dragons had devoted more firepower to this battle than any since last time the Shadow Lords had come out to wreak havoc.

Switching topics, I said, "I understand why I'd go after Dariyah. She is my mate, and we are joined. Her fate will eventually become mine."

"You're wondering what my stake in this is, eh?"

I'd been questing about for a neutral way to pose the question. He'd just saved me the trouble. "Are you going to tell me?"

"The two of you are not only bound to one another but to dragonkind. If we do not save Dariyah, eventually her absence will drill a hole into every dragon's soul."

"Why did you do that? Why take a chance on us? Dragons have never aligned with those outside their own ranks before."

"'Twas a point of contention," Ash admitted. "The seers prevailed. If we'd chosen a different path, we'd have faced a different set of issues."

I didn't expect him to clarify what those issues might have been, and he didn't.

"Where are we going first?" I asked.

"The most likely spot. Where we thought the Shadow Lords would remain until the end of time."

Nothing but to wait out the journey spell. Facing down evil in its lair seemed like a fool's errand with only two of us. Not that we weren't strong magically. My ribs had nearly healed, which meant I'd have full access to my power for fighting. And we'd be three counting Dariyah.

"If you do not trust me," Ash went on, "feel free to return to Faery and the battle."

"Because I ask questions doesn't mean I don't trust you," I told him firmly. "The more I know, the better prepared I'll be for what we face." Since he probably didn't know—or perhaps he did—I added, "The reason there are so many Unseelie is because someone cloned them. Probably the Gorgons or Shadow Lords."

The dragon turned to face me once more, head swiveling atop his long, sinuous neck. "Cloned, as in made copies?"

"Aye, exactly."

"How is that even possible?"

I considered his question. Clearly, it hadn't been finessed in a modern lab with petri dishes and agar plates and incubators. "I'm not certain, but I assume someone used magic to create mirror images of Unseelie mages. And not only a single copy, multiple ones."

Breath hissed through my teeth. I hadn't realized I'd clenched my jaws together. "I asked Shade, the mage who told me, why they'd tolerated such a personal affront."

"What did he say?"

"That they'd had no choice. Between the Gorgons and Shadow Lords, it was foisted upon them."

"Does anyone else know?"

"Aye, I told Auril. She and Ysir are searching for a way to do away with the copies. Anything created with magic—"

"Can be destroyed by the same," Ash finished my thought. "Good. I wish them luck. They should pull dragons into their quest."

"I'm certain they will," I said, even though I wasn't sure of anything.

"We're nearly there," Ash said. "Ward yourself."

"Not going to do that. If we face Shadow Lords, they'll slice right through my warding, and I'll have squandered power for nothing. Better to throw everything I have into fighting."

A barren world took shape around us. I thought it looked a lot like Fire Mountain with cracked dirt extending in all directions, but I didn't give voice to my thought for fear of offending Ash. No volcanoes here, and only a single relentless sun hanging low on the horizon. I scanned for life, any at all, and came up dry.

"No one is here," I said, fully expecting the dragon to launch another journey spell. We were wasting time.

"Look closer," Ash said. "Beneath us, not around us." He took off at a surprisingly brisk pace given we were on the ground. Heat from his scaly hide, which hadn't been as noticeable while we were in the void between worlds, seared me through ripped spots in my trousers.

The plain we'd been on gave way to rolling land. Still dry, dusty, and not sporting so much as a bush, I wondered if this place had ever supported life. A hole in the ground grew larger as we approached it.

"Do you sense Dariyah?" I asked pointblank because I didn't.

"Not sure. Off me," Ash said.

I vaulted to the ground and ran to the edge of the chasm. When I got close, I saw crumbling steps leading downward. The space would accommodate me, but not Ash. "I'll report back," I told the dragon and started down the stairs.

"I have a different route in mind," the dragon said.

I stopped about twenty steps down and turned. "Don't bother until I see if anyone is down here."

"There is."

But was it Dariyah? I wasn't willing to spin my

wheels here for any other reason. At least I hadn't picked up the putrid reek of Shadow Lords.

Backwash from the dragon's power buffeted me; I raised a mage light to illuminate my way and hurtled downward. The steps switched from a straight shot to a spiral. Someone had gone to a lot of trouble to build this access point. Caution rocketed to the fore, and I swathed myself in a ward. Quick jabs of seeking magic suggested Ash had been correct. Something alive was down here. Why hadn't I sensed it from the surface?

Something, but not Dariyah.

The bottom rose up to meet me sooner than I expected. A dank, dirt corridor stretched ahead with metal doors scribed into both sides. Before I walked between a set of doors, I stretched power ahead of me: testing, checking. I wouldn't do anyone any good if I blundered into a trap. Iron erodes magic, and my skin tingled from the bite of it. Ash had said he'd meet me, but he wouldn't fit down here. Nothing reacted to the threads of magic I'd forced ahead, so I edged forward, no longer expecting to be hit by enemy crossfire.

A low moan from behind the first door stopped me dead. Damn if this wasn't a dungeon designed by mages to keep others like them captive. I tried a shot of magic through the door, but it bounced back at me. "Who are you?" I called softly. If jailers were anywhere near, I hadn't seen any evidence of them.

"Who are you?" a strident female voice called back.

All the other prisoners heard the exchange because a cacophony of voices rioted through the underground enclosure.

"Not why we're here. Move quickly, all the way to the end." I'd started for the nearest door to see if I couldn't free whoever was within, but Ash's harsh words brought me up short.

I bolted toward the sound of his voice, passing at least twenty doors before I traded the cellblock for a large, open space lit by Ash's innate glow. Suspended near the middle behind rows of what looked like glowing barbed wire was Dariyah. Her hands had been lashed to hooks hanging in the air. Magic supported them. Blood trickled down her arms, and she groaned.

Breath hissed from me. She was alive. It was the only thing that mattered.

I darted forward, intent on joining my power with Ash's to free her, but Pegasus pranced between us. "Not so fast, Cynwrigg ap Llyr. She is mine. More mine than she'll ever be yours. Leave this place."

"Think again." I spat the words and readied myself to fight. One dragon. One winged horse. Add me to the equation, and it wouldn't be much of a contest. I reached out intent on igniting my link to Dariyah, but it was as if whoever hung there wasn't her.

"What have you done?" I demanded.

"How much is it worth to you...Regent?" Pegasus taunted me.

"I know precisely what he did," Ash said in his deep, gravelly voice. "We must proceed carefully, or we'll lose her for good."

## CHAPTER FIFTEEN, DARIYAH

**W**hen Pegasus made a grab for me, I was certain I could defeat him. After all, I had my own power plus Cyn's and dragonkind's on tap. Ha. That little fantasy blew up in my face as the horse carved through my warding as if it didn't exist and snatched me between his front hoofs.

I cycled through a bunch of spells, ladling out power words as if they didn't cost me—except they did. Nothing altered the grip of those razor-sharp hoofs on my upper arms. He cut through my clothes, and it felt like knives carving through my triceps.

Since magic wasn't working, I switched to words mostly to allow my power to recover for another volley. "Where are you taking me?"

"She speaks." He mocked me, and it got my dander

up. I might be helpless at the moment, but he couldn't keep me trapped between his front legs forever.

"Nah. I'm dumb as a post. That would be your half of the gene pool."

A sharp nip from his squared off teeth grazed the top of my head. I tried a different tack. "What do you want with me? You wouldn't exactly have qualified for any father-of-the-year awards."

"I didn't know about you," he informed me tartly.

"Even if you had," I retorted, "nothing would have changed."

Horsey laughter grated against my ears. "Oh but it would," he said. "I'd have cut you out of Auril's womb before you were more than a collection of cells."

"Smart of her not to offer you that opportunity." Honey dripped from my statement.

"Inconsiderate," he corrected me.

My turn to laugh. I tried for carefree, but it wasn't happening with pain rolling through both arms. "Men. You're all the same once your dicks get hard. Putty in our hands."

His hoofs cut deeper. I'd hit a nerve. "Not the first time said dick has gotten you into trouble?" I inquired in saccharine tones.

"None of your affair. Did no one teach you respect?"

"Mother tried, but it's probably a lost cause at this point. Where are you taking me?"

"Somewhere you'll be for a long time. Somewhere no one can find you."

My bond with Cyn and the dragons began to stretch on the heels of his words. I moved fast, slathered power around the shared spot in my magical center doing my damnedest to protect it. We sparred with each other for a tense handful of moments. Maybe I'd win this round.

The bond shrieked in protest, a sound probably only I could hear, before it cleaved in two and I lost my connection with Cyn and the dragons. Pain cascaded through me, far worse than the edges of Pegasus's hoofs. Deeper than physical, the agony of loss would have doubled me over if I hadn't been clutched between the horse's forelegs.

"Like I said, no one will ever find you," Pegasus neighed raucously.

After that, I retreated into myself layering power to close everything I could from his incursions. I felt him probing my mind, working to peel it like the layers of an onion. So far, I was keeping him at bay, but my magic wouldn't last forever. Not without a source to replenish it.

"Your name," Pegasus growled, an unusual sound coming from a horse.

"Dariyah," I tossed out.

"No. That is not your name. Tell me what I want to know, or I will pulverize your puny brain."

I laughed again, long and bitter. Mother's insistence had saved me from myself—again. "Lots of luck," I said when I could talk. "I have no idea what my true name is."

The blackness around us ceded to yet one more world. I'd sure as fuck seen a whole lot of them lately. A featureless plain stretched on all sides of us. If there was water here, it wasn't apparent. Long fissures split the parched earth. Pegasus had let go of me; I wanted to rub feeling back into my abraded arms, but wouldn't give him the pleasure of knowing he'd hurt me. Instead, I sent threads of magic to heal my hurt places, grateful when power answered my summons. I hadn't been sure it would in this place.

"Walk," he ordered.

I glanced up at him. "We could fly."

"We could, except I told you to walk." He lashed out with a hind leg, but I jumped out of the way before it connected. I was heartily sick of being his whipping girl.

Borrowing a page from a brief stint I'd had on stage, I turned in a full circle. "Gee. Everything looks the same. Does it matter which way?"

"No. This is my realm."

Interesting. I'd had no idea Pegasus even had a world, and I'd forgotten about Medusa's until she dragged me there. Crap. Mother could have picked a better family to marry into. From what I'd seen of my father and in-laws, they were a pack of losers. Amused by overlaying what was normal for everyone else onto my deucedly abnormal situation, I picked a direction and started walking. Not too fast. I didn't want him to believe he'd cowed me.

"I figured out which one your mother was," Pegasus said.

"So?"

"It's not nice to masquerade as a mortal," he went on.

I stopped and twisted to face him. "Not nice? You just kidnapped me. That falls into way worse than the 'not nice' category. Besides, you were playing at being a mortal that night too. Or maybe it was high noon. I have no idea when the two of you got together. Mother hid the circumstances of my birth from me until they caught up with her."

It's tough to interpret horse expressions, but something that might have been surprise flitted across his snout, and he flicked his ears. "Why would she have hidden such a thing from you?"

I snorted. "Probably because she was ashamed." So long as I was being provocative, I kept on with it. "You were a vehicle for her to bring a series of prophecies to life. Mother is a seer, first and foremost. She became the Queen of Air and Darkness at a later date."

"What prophecy?" He pawed the cracked earth with a hoof.

I shrugged. "You shanghaied the wrong woman. It's a question for her. Or one of the dragon seers. They seem to know the lay of the land too."

Power shot from him and wrapped me in something that burned like fire. "You will tell me."

"Impossible since I don't have the whole story. I'm an instrument of fate, as were you. Live with it." My last bit of bravado was forced, but I was weary of him and his supercilious attitude.

Apparently, he was just as done with me as I was with him. So much for a cozy father-daughter reunion. Heat seared me from all sides, but I couldn't see flames or smell smoke. What manner of power did that? I was used to magefire and dragonfire, but his non-fire created ungodly pain that moved from my sides inward until I was squeezed nearly in two. Breath came in little panting gasps. I clenched my jaws tight, not willing to give him the satisfaction of hearing me scream.

I must have blacked out because when consciousness flickered, flirting with me, I was in a dimly lit, rounded enclosure. The smell of damp earth suggested we'd moved underground. With a great deal of effort, I scanned for details. Others were in this area. Many others despite me not being able to see them. Their misery was palpable.

"I sense mages not far from here. What did you do to them?" I rasped.

"They are my pets. A far more pertinent question is what I plan to do with you."

Finally. He was right about something. I'd wasted a whole lot of time when I should have been pulling out all the stops to escape. But I hadn't expected him to overreact to my insults, either. In theory, we were both long past grown-up. Meant we had thick skins and could engage in a bit of name calling in the interest of baiting one another. Sort of like foreplay, except he was skipping to the main event.

Probably no one had ever challenged him before.

"What are your plans?" I asked sweetly. "I'm all ears."

"I'm afraid you're a day late and a dollar short, my dear."

I'd have taunted him about borrowing jargon from humans, but fear lit a fire under me. It added urgency to the one burning me from all sides. I gave up on subtlety. Gathering everything in me, I initiated a leap out of this place. And fell flat on my face. Maybe I didn't believe hard enough. More likely, I didn't have enough power left. We scuffled, and he dragged me by the scruff of the neck. Anyone who ever described horse teeth as dull hasn't felt them up close and personal. After my third break for freedom, I ended up impaled on hooks that hung in the air like a perverse imitation of Christ's cross minus the nails.

My hands stung and ached. Blood dribbled down my

wrists and arms. While I writhed in agony and plotted revenge, Pegasus drove a stake dead center into the reservoir that holds my power; magic poured from me. I was helpless to staunch the flow, just like I'd been after I started to close the rift beneath Faery.

Faery hadn't meant me ill. At worst, she was oblivious. Pegasus played by a whole different rulebook.

Suspended, helpless, everything that defined me drained to nothing in this goddess-be-damned cave. Voices buffeted my third ear. Some laughing, others howling. Finally, one did something other than yowl. *"So you're the latest, eh?"* a woman's voice rasped. *"Maybe we'll be cellmates."*

*"What do you mean?"*

*"You'll find out. But you really stepped in it this time, sweetie."*

*"What are you?"* I asked, almost not wanting to know.

*"Once I was Fae. Now I am nothing."*

"See?" Pegasus sounded ungodly proud of being a rogue. "She understands. You will too. You'll be my special one. For a while. No one lasts, though."

I focused on him with more difficulty that I'd thought possible. "Except you?" I growled.

"Aye. Except me," he agreed cheerily. His head twisted around, and he tilted it as if he were listening. "Oh good. The rescue committee is here. Looks as if I'm about to host my very first dragon. Mother would be so proud."

"Still trying to please Mommy dearest?" I jeered just before he blanketed me in something that made my head spin. Consciousness took a hike. When it returned I figured I was hallucinating because Cyn and Ash were here. I tried to say something but had no voice. It took a moment before I understood the part of me that was still sentient was my astral self. My physical body barely clung to life, eyes shut, breathing shallowly a few feet beneath where I hovered.

Ash said something about losing me forever. It should have scared the bejesus out of me. Instead, a weary calm descended. If this was how everything ground to a halt, I'd come to terms with it. Somehow.

It wasn't as if I had a choice in the matter.

I tried to kick myself out of my inertia; nothing changed. I'd been in similar situations before where my astral self had detached from my body, but then I'd been in control. Pegasus had done something to force the split. I had no magic left, but no one was paying any attention to me.

Ash and Cyn were telling Pegasus if he didn't restore me immediately, they'd make sure he never flew another kilometer because the dragon would incinerate his pretty wings.

I flitted nearer my body, ready to bounce out of

reach, but I didn't have to. The men were fully engaged in dick-waving. Thank the mother goddess for testosterone, the original one-track-mind chemical. Because I was spirit, the best I could do was send air currents against the spot Pegasus had drilled into my reservoir. It was enough. The other me, the real one, heaved a sigh. The enchanted spike riddled with evil popped out, and the hole it had made began to seal over.

Did this world have a way to replenish my power? I had no idea, but Pegasus had identified it as his home base. Presumably, it refueled him. His mother may have been a monster, but his father was Poseidon, god of the seas. The magic might be a close-enough match to help me regroup.

Fire shot from Ash's open jaws, scribing its way around one of the horse's wings. The smell of burning feathers was thick, cloying. Pegasus took to the air, neighing furiously. Ash sprang right behind him, intent on adding fire to the horse's other wing. Dragon wings are scaled, so they're impervious to fire. Good plan on someone's part since aerial firefights are where they live.

Crap. I might be spirit, but my mind was all over the fucking place. A quick check of the rest of me was encouraging. A smidgeon of magic had resurrected itself now that it wasn't draining out as fast as it formed. Cyn was cutting through the magical equivalent of electrified barbed wire, intent on getting to my body.

When had Pegasus set all those barriers in place? Maybe I'd been unconscious longer than I thought. He must have had materials at the ready. Yeah. That had to be it. Not his first rodeo capturing someone. Look at all those people who'd tried to talk with me when I was still whole.

I wasn't doing any good here. The horse and dragon were roaring and filling the air with burning feathers, fire, and ashy smoke. Cyn would be a while snipping cables and not having them snap back and beat him half to death. I pushed toward where the voices had come from.

It's hard to put any kind of distance between spirit and body, so the farther away I moved, the slower I was. Finally, a rounded corridor opened off the cave and a row of cells came into view. Fuck. Pegasus was even more of an abomination than his mother.

The first two cells were about as far as I'd be able to go. *"Who are all of you?"* I might not have a real voice, but I could still manage mind speech.

Many answers battered me. Evidently, these were all manner of mage, ones who'd pissed Pegasus off. *"Why haven't you tried to escape?"*

A single word, *"Iron,"* echoed and re-echoed.

*"It will sting,"* I told them. *"A lot. But it won't kill you. If all of you make a break for it at the same time, the discomfort should be mitigated because it will be spread amongst you."*

A roar rose. What had I loosed? Too late now. I was about to find out, but I was banking on the old saying about the enemy of my enemy being my friend. The band stretching between me and my body yanked so hard I yelped. Didn't matter. No voice, so no one heard me.

Cyn had worked his way through the charged wire to my body. He'd freed one hand from the hook, but the full weight of my body hung from the other one. Cyn tried to support me from below. It helped, a little. I tried to reenter my body, expecting it to be straightforward. It wasn't. Something blocked my path. The corporeal part of me cried out. Working on instinct, no doubt driven by excruciating pain, I'd managed to unhook myself using my newly free hand. I dropped to the ground in a crumpled heap.

A thud whipped my attention to one side. Pegasus's wings had burned to nubs. He was working on growing new ones; meanwhile, he'd fallen out of the sky. Ash landed on top of him, spraying every horsey inch with dragonfire.

"Wait," someone cried. "Don't kill him."

"Aye, save him for us," another person screeched.

"We want a piece of that action," someone else chimed in.

The prisoners streamed into the cave. They were filthy with matted hair and clothing that had nearly rotted off from their lengthy captivity, but long-shut-tered magic shimmered around them. Fae. Sidhe. Nymphs. Even a unicorn. How in the hell had Poseidon captured one of them?

Ash obligingly climbed off the winged horse. Those he'd wronged piled on. Grateful I'd been able to help despite the absence of a body, I turned my attention to the problem at hand.

Cyn kept a protective arm around my shoulders. He'd pulled me to my feet, and he was the only thing keeping me upright. He probed, doing his damnedest to reestablish his link with me, but of course I wasn't whole.

Ash lumbered over dusting his scaled forelegs together. "That was satisfying," he announced.

"For me as well. That one's demise is no loss to the world. What's wrong with Dariyah?" Cynwrigg asked. "You said you knew."

"I do. Her spirit is there." He angled his neck my way. "Pegasus snatched it from her body and then barred it from returning."

The pack of mages had all but obliterated Pegasus's burning form. None had weapons, but they sliced and diced with various enchantments until bits of the horse flew into the air. Anger is a marvelous tool in and of itself, particularly when augmented by a mix of magics.

"I've never heard of such a thing. How can we fix it?"

Cyn angled his burnished metal gaze at the dragon. I edged closer to my body, still seeking a way inside.

The dragon's magic scoured me, digging deep. I didn't feel it, but my body flinched under the onslaught. Fanning his wings, he spun to face the mass of bodies arrayed over Pegasus. "Hold," he thundered and trudged to the fallen horse.

Grumbling, reluctant, the mages fell back, opening a path for him.

"He's still alive," a nymph warned.

"And a very good thing for his daughter," Ash replied.

"Daughter? We had no idea he had such a thing." The nymph made a sour face. "Poor dear. What a curse to labor under."

Ash sliced through what was left of the horse's neck up by his head. A glittering golden ball detached itself. With more delicacy than I'd have thought the dragon capable of, he captured the fragile orb, cradling it gently in a palm, and walked toward me. When he got close, he told Cyn, "Open this with that blade of yours, but very carefully. Pegasus stole a bit of Dariyah's essence and mixed it with his own. 'Twas how he intended to tether her to him. Once it's free, she'll be whole again."

I'll never know what tipped Ash off, how he understood what to do, but Cyn balanced the orb in his hand. It vibrated gently, but it wouldn't live for long separated from its owner. Blade at the ready, he nicked the slightest hole in one end of the globe. A stream of white light jetted into my body, followed by me snapping into place.

Breath whistled from my lungs. My eyes fluttered open, and I regarded Cynwrigg and the dragon as relief crashed through me. "I never want to do that again," I gasped, shocked by how rusty my voice sounded.

"You never should have let him capture you in the first place." Ash extended a talon toward me.

"Tell me something I don't know. I kept expecting to fight him. Mother told me facing him in armed combat was why I'd been born."

Ash shook his big head. Scales rattled. "What she told you was you held the key to an event that would take him down. You assumed it meant a battle, but prophecies have many unexpected twists and turns."

Talk about understatements. Somewhere between a twist and a turn, I'd nearly lost my way. "Who in the hell were all those prisoners?"

"No time to find out now, but they're free," Cyn said.

"I did that. Or my astral self did," I murmured. "Told them how to pile their efforts together to bypass the iron. None of them were locked in."

Ash trumpeted. Some of the mages, who'd moved from killing to eating their tormentor, glanced up. "Can you get yourselves home from here?" Ash asked.

"Aye. Thank you," a Sidhe replied.

"Do not tarry," Ash told them. "If I were you, I'd leave right away."

I was still getting my bearings, letting it sink in I wasn't going to breathe my last in this shithole when Ash tumbled me onto his back with a welcome shot of dragon power. Somehow, the wound in my magical center was repairing itself, but it would be a while before I could do more than kindle a mage light.

Cyn landed behind me and placed his arms around my shoulders, crushing the sides of my wings. It didn't hurt, and I leaned into his embrace. "How's the war going?"

"No idea," he replied tersely.

"Which is why we have to get back there now," Ash said. "Medusa must know her son is dead. I'm expecting her and maybe her Gorgon kinswomen to show up any moment."

"But that's a good thing," I protested. "If they're here, then they're not killing us off in Faery."

"A good thing for now," the dragon cautioned me, "but hell hath no fury like a mother grieving a child. Medusa will come after us for today, and she'll leverage all the evil she can find to aid her."

The cavern dropped away; the place I was bonded with Cyn and the dragons ignited again, humming with a warm glow. Maybe I hadn't had sufficient magic to support it until now. Cyn tucked my head into the hollow between his neck and shoulder. "I am so glad today had a decent ending. When I felt our linkage shatter, I..."

"Yeah. I know. When Pegasus severed it, I knew I was in trouble, but I underestimated him. He's nothing like Oberon."

"Nay, he isn't," Cyn agreed. "Faery's king used to have a few saving graces. Pegasus has always been evil through and through. Those poor prisoners."

"Looked as if most of them had been here for quite a while," I muttered.

"It's how he strengthened his magic," Ash spoke up. "He drained them. It was why he required so many because the ones he drank from needed many months to come back up to snuff."

"You make him sound like a vampire," I said.

"In some respects he was, except his preferred beverage was magic, not blood."

The Midnight Court shimmered into being around us. It was quiet, devoid of anyone. I could sleep for days, but we had work to do.

"Are you all right?" Cyn asked.

"If licking the bottom of a parakeet cage is defined as all right, then yeah, I'm peachy. Let's do this. Mother said three battles. Fingers crossed we ended up on top in this one."

Thinking about Mother brought her on a run. She

sprang through a gash in the air. "Goddess be praised. You're back. No time to waste." Snatching me out of Cyn's arms, she poured magic into me, so much and so fast that for a moment it was tough to catch my breath.

"What's happened?" Ash asked.

"We've entered the endgame," Mother replied. "Things could go either way." She narrowed her eyes. "Pegasus is dead, isn't he?" At my nod, she went on. "It may aid us. The Gorgons are gone. All of them."

"They'll be back soon enough," the dragon said. "Once they discover naught can be done to resurrect him."

"Are you certain of that?" Mother arched both brows.

"Of course not." Cyn stepped in. "Magic doesn't work that way. But if bleeding out, losing your power, and being set upon by a pack of angry mages will do the trick, we're golden."

"Where'd they come from?" Mother asked.

"They were his prisoners and how he restored his power," I said. "When we left, they were eating his remains."

Mother cracked a rare smile. "This is getting better and better. All right. Let's hit it."

I've rarely felt less like "hitting" anything, but we had to be close. To something. No rest for the weary. Or the wicked. Or anyone else it appeared. The familiar feel of

Cyn's power snatched me up and deposited me in our usual spot behind Dubrova.

Between my brief respite and Mother's hasty infusion of magic I almost felt whole. Almost. "Buck up," I mumbled in an approximation of a pep talk.

"What?" Cyn asked.

"Nothing. Let's get this over with."

## CHAPTER SIXTEEN, CYN

Weariness streamed from Dariyah in waves. I'd have insisted she sit this one out, but Auril's summons was impossible to deny. Even if I'd tried, though, I doubt if anything I could have said would have driven her from the field. She was strong, a trouper. When she'd been hanging right in front of me In Pegasus's lair, and I hadn't been able to sense her with magic, I'd been ready to tear the world apart to bring her back to me. Except I'd have blundered around and still not thought to examine Pegasus's magical center. I owed the dragon a debt I could never repay, but I'd do my damnedest to be there if he needed me.

First, we had to get through the rest of today, except it was tomorrow. Day had ceded to night, which had come and gone. Dawn was upon us. A gnarly one with red streaks painting the horizon.

I smelled the battle before it lurched into focus around us. Blood and guts and the ozone reek of expended magic floated beneath that surreal, macabre sky. Where was Faery? Damn it. I hadn't thought about her until right now. Ideally, I should have tried for a connection before leaving the Midnight Court.

Auril stood next to me, hand shading her eyes as she surveyed what had once been verdant grounds around a graceful castle. "Have you heard from Faery?" I asked.

"She's done a few things." Auril's tone suggested the land could have done a whole lot more.

"I'm going to see what's left of my troop," Dariyah said.

"No!" Auril's voice was even sharper than normal, which was saying a lot. "All of us must stay together for what remains of this battle. The soldiers have found their way without us, most particularly without you since you've been gone so long."

"Your edict doesn't include me," Ash said. "I will be with the other dragons." Wings rustled as he jumped skyward, nimble for all his bulk.

"It did," Auril shouted after him, but he kept on flying.

Titania and Ysir joined us. I hadn't seen where they came from. Dirt and blood tracked down their faces;

their clothing was torn. Gritty determination etched into their features. "Oberon?" I looked from one to the other and got head shakes.

"He never was overly gutsy," Titania said. "Today's been a wee bit on the bloody side. More like him to wait till everything is over and then craft whatever perfidy he has in mind."

Ysir shook his head again. "Nay, we will not see him for a while."

"How can you be certain?" I wasn't keen on looking over my shoulder for Oberon to jump me. I was his logical target, the body standing between him and reclaiming Faery's throne. I wasn't exactly firing on all cylinders, but the thought was timely.

"We need a line of succession," I said. "In case something happens to me."

"Already handled," Titania retorted. "It begins with me, travels to Ysir, and then to Ulane."

"Is that written down somewhere?" I asked.

"Not exactly, but the birds at the Midnight Court know," Ysir replied. "And the court voted on it through a series of hawk messengers."

It would have to be sufficient. Every muscle in my body ached. My bones weren't far behind. I could imagine how Dariyah fared. She'd been through more than I had.

"What happened with the clones?" I asked.

"Gone." Ysir dusted his filthy palms together. "Once we knew what to look for, it was simple enough to identify the ones who'd been created."

"Aye, after a few experiments, we ended up batching them. Quicker that way," Auril added.

I wasn't certain what she meant but explanations could wait. Breath rushed from me at the unexpected but very welcome news. "Strong work."

"Why thank you." Auril mimed a bow.

Dariyah turned to her mother. "I want to know about who cloned what, but not now. Tell us how this next part will roll out."

"We enter Dubrova and battle the Shadow Lords. If they leave, the Unseelie won't be far behind."

My spine cracked as I squared my shoulders. It wasn't the answer I'd been anticipating. "How will we do that?"

A spell settled over the five of us. Auril spoke into our minds. As her strategy unfolded, I was impressed. It was bold, unprecedented, and it just might work. We'd need the dragons, though. I almost hated to ask them for anything else, but they were an elemental part of our defenses.

"Does Faery play a role?" I inquired before Auril broke the warding shielding us from prying ears.

"She does. Whether she will show up and do her part remains to be seen." Auril paused before directing her next words at the land. "I don't know if you're listening. This is an opportunity to redeem yourself and save your world. If you fail us, you fail yourself."

The place I held a bond with the land vibrated with emotion. Maybe outrage, maybe shame. I couldn't interpret it, but I turned my mind voice her way. *"I have faith in you."*

*"Good to know someone does."* Her bitter reply told me she'd been listening to everything.

"She'll be there," I told everyone just before Auril's enchantment dissipated. No reason to tarry. The next spell spit us out in the cellars beneath Dubrova. Once, they'd housed dungeons and an extensive wine cellar. The sour smell of spilled wine told me someone had pulled the plugs on many of the casks.

"The dragons are in place," Auril said tersely.

I began a countdown. Their job was diversionary. They'd attack from the air, drawing attention upward and setting fire to anything left that would burn. We started for the stairs winding to Dubrova's main floor. It was still intact. I instructed myself not to look at a place I'd once loved, my home for all the years of my long life. Even if we won, rebuilding Dubrova was scarcely a priority.

Reaching for Dariyah, I gripped her hand and married my magic to hers. We were far stronger joined like this. She and I went first with Ysir behind us and the sisters behind him. The configuration maximized our combined—and divergent—magics.

As Auril had hoped, the first floor was empty. All the Unseelie were in the field. Thank all the gods they'd been reduced to normal numbers courtesy of Ysir and Auril.

And me. If I hadn't killed Timmons twice, I'd never have thought to ask the questions that led to a discovery that might make a significant difference.

"Ready yourselves." Auril fanned right, and we formed a single line, magic at the ready.

"You dare enter our domain?" a disembodied voice echoed off the walls.

"Sorry," I called out, "but this was my realm last I checked."

"Look again, Regent. Events have a way of changing." A tall robed form floated into the castle great room. His cowl hid his face and the robe every other part of him. Was there even a body beneath it? They weren't called Shadow Lords for nothing.

Power crackled around the figure. Jagged bursts of black lightning fed off one another.

"Where are your brethren?" Auril asked.

"Attending to our Unseelie allies." A growl emanated from within his cowl. "What is left of them."

"Cheaters never win," Dariyah said cheerily and spread her wings. "Daddy's dead too. So sad. Too bad."

The growl deepened, sounding more and more feral. Shadow Lords were once men, fallen kings and queens. What in the hell had happened to this one? "Leave here now," he repeated, extending an arm.

I looked for a hand, but nothing stuck out from the end of the full sleeve. Feeling stupid because I hadn't bothered to check before, I circled the figure with seeking magic and drew the noose up tight. Sure enough, it closed on empty air.

"Illusion," I shouted. "And projection."

"Where the fuck are they?" Dariyah demanded and kindled seeking magic of her own.

Suddenly, I thought I knew. "Faery! Watch yourself," I shouted, not bothering with telepathy. On the heels of my words, a deep rumble shook the floor beneath our feet.

"Time to leave." Auril took off running for where the front doors had been. They were still there, but canted at crazy angles and half off their hinges.

We burst through in time to see rocks explode upward from a rapidly forming crater between the castle and the moat. Stone gnashing against stone was so loud I directed magic to shield my ears. Dariyah extended her wings and flew upward, probably to get a better look.

"On your left," she shrieked.

I spun to face another robed figure, this one with hands, feet, and a face so skeletal it was the stuff of night terrors. No time to experiment, so I picked a water-heavy spell and heaved it at my adversary expecting it to bounce off him. Surely, he was warded. Instead, it covered him in a wave. Blisters formed on his skin, and he launched himself right at me. I'd hurt him, but not badly enough. Auril, Titania, and Ysir were set upon as well.

Dariyah rained lethal enchantment laced with fire and earth from above.

We'd never known how many Shadow Lords there were. I'd thought perhaps six, but at least a dozen blew through the hole Faery had formed. Clearly, she'd known where they were hidden and targeted their lair.

*"Thank you."* I sent the thought her way.

*"Thank me in person,"* she said and blasted out of the same gap she'd pushed the Shadow Lords through.

They mobbed us, lobbing darts that formed festering sores where they connected. I ignored the first one, but it was a mistake. The wound swelled, spewing putrid pus until I directed healing magic to counteract it. Even with the full brunt of my healing efforts, bone was showing before I defeated the Shadow Lord's poison.

I'd pushed the poison-monger back a few feet, but hadn't damaged him that I could tell. Dariyah landed next to me and added her magic to patching up my hand. "Looks bad," she said.

"I'll live. I liked it better when you were flying."

"Except nothing I was doing made a difference."

Dragons massed above us, showering the courtyard with smoke and flames.

Three Shadow Lords rushed right at Dariyah and me. My blade jumped into my uninjured hand, and I swung it not expecting much. If decapitation could have done away with these bastards, they wouldn't be here today. The push-pull of bone and sinew caught at the edges of my sword. I sawed through with a magical assist and made it to the other side.

I expected the fucker's head to roll onto the ground. Instead, it bounced a couple of times on his neck and reattached. Not a drop of blood fell when there should have been buckets from severed vessels.

"They're dead," Dariyah snarled.

"Makes getting rid of them a whole lot harder," I shouted back.

"Do you think garlic and holy water would do the trick? Or a stake through the heart?" Fanning the air with her wings, she flew out of reach of a pair who'd tried to grab her, kicking one squarely in the jaw. I heard the crunch of bones breaking, but it didn't slow him down. He jumped and almost caught hold of Dariyah's booted foot.

Almost doesn't count.

Dragonfire burned holes in robes, but for some reason the material didn't catch. Not much else burnable down here, but the dragons kept trying. A green one grabbed one of the Shadow Lords in his taloned forelegs, flew about a hundred feet above the ground, and dropped him. After a moment when I hoped it would at least knock the wind out of his undead lungs, he lurched to his feet and dove back into the fray.

Auril was holding her own. Titania fought next to Faery. Ysir had jumped atop one of Dubrova's broken walls. So much magic gushed from him he'd taken on a blue glow. Apparently, he'd dealt some crippling strikes because the Shadow Lords gave him a wide berth.

Faery strode forward, spread her arms wide, and cried, "You will leave my realm. Never return."

"But you invited us." One of the robed figures stopped a couple of feet in front of her.

My heart lurched; my stomach curdled into a knot. Faery had betrayed us. She wasn't refuting his statement. Not right away like I'd have expected her to address a boldfaced lie.

"You think so?" She advanced until she was inches from him. "'Twasn't me but Oberon who invited you. As I recall the progression of events, he invited the Unseelie. Their king is who suggested you tag along. You and the Gorgons and Medusa's spawn."

"Details." The Shadow Lord shrugged. "We are here now. We have claimed this world as our own. Once we do that, we never leave."

"Unclaim it," Faery's words were silky, but their meaning wasn't.

"Sorry."

"Aye, you will be sorry. Very sorry." Faery smirked. Any similarity to something mortal departed. Her eyes gleamed dangerously, growing large and luminous. She gripped the Shadow Lord's shoulders with long fingers that turned into claws. Ripping chunks from the dead body, she tossed them aside, but they bounced back toward their master in an attempt to be whole again.

"I don't think so," Dariyah snarled. Picking up some of the pieces, she chucked them into a pile and scuttled off to one side. The dragon seers strafed the spot, pouring fire on the chunks until a greasy fire began to burn. It stank of rot and decay. Dariyah chucked more of the embattled Shadow Lord onto the pyre. Finally, it burned brighter but didn't smell any better.

With a wrenching, cracking noise, Faery twisted the Shadow Lord's head off and threw it to Dariyah, who dropped it into the fire. Once it was burning, what was left of the robed form crumpled to the ground.

"Come on." Faery curled her claws into a parody of a come-hither gesture. "That was fun. I'd welcome another victim."

The Shadow Lords who'd jumped me, doing their level best to drill through my warding with their poison, shuffled back. Had it registered that their dead state couldn't protect them from Faery's wrath?

The dragons scudded heavily to earth, forming a rough circle around what had been Dubrova's courtyard. "Leave," Ash bellowed.

"Why should we?" another of the Shadow Lords skinned his lips back from a row of rotten teeth.

The dragon didn't answer. He snapped his jaws, and a spinning vortex powered by dragon enchantment formed out of Faery's air. The Shadow Lords scrambled to craft an exit spell, but they were too late. Ash's maelstrom scooped them into its maw. When it cleared, they were gone.

"We'll see if they stay away this time," he rumbled around smoke and ash streaming from his open jaws.

Dariyah trudged next to me. Ysir jumped down from his perch. Auril and Titania joined us. A celebration was in order, but I'd never felt less like celebrating. We'd sustained losses. I had no idea how many, but I'd prioritize finding out, caring for the injured, and honoring our dead.

"The Unseelie are withdrawing," Faery said, a wicked grin splitting her alien features into something unrecognizable. "I knew they would. The King of Winter hates to lose."

"They'll regroup and return," Auril replied. "It won't take them all that long. Medusa will be out for blood, and she'll have her sisters and Chrysaor with her."

"Nicely done, my dears." A familiar voice preceded Oberon's appearance. Unlike the rest of us, he looked as if he'd just stepped from a state dinner with pristine robes and not a speck of battle dirt in sight.

"Get lost," Titania growled.

"Is that any way to greet your husband?" He adopted an expression I remembered well. One I'd thought endearing at a very long ago point in time.

"You stopped being my husband when you dropped me in that hellhole for fifty years." Titania flapped her hands his way. "Leave. There is no place for you here."

"Of course there is," he purred and sidled closer to Faery. "You have your body back because of me, my dear. Surely, you'll reconsider and offer me the land link once again."

Faery tossed her head back and laughed so hard her gold-and-silver hair danced around her shoulders.

"But your body." Oberon tried again. He'd been confident when he'd waltzed into our midst, but his veneer had developed cracks.

"Little enough recompense for the damage you sowed." She skewered him with her gaze until he was forced to look away.

"If you do not leave"—Ash took a step forward—"we will imprison you in Fire Mountain's dungeons."

"You can't do that. I'm the king of Faery," he bristled.

"Not anymore, you aren't," I said and left it at that. Reminding him of all the chances he'd had to act like a king worthy of the title would be a waste of breath.

Looking as shabby as the rest of us, the King of Winter shimmered into being next to Oberon. It took him a few tries before he was fully corporeal, which suggested his power had run down to bedrock. Good. I hoped it never fully recovered.

"We will leave—for now." The King of Winter tilted his chin defiantly. "But we shall return. You'll not see us coming, and next time—"

"We'll conquer you again." I drowned out the rest of his words with mine.

Over Oberon's garbled protests, the Unseelie king's spell snared them both. I hoped their destination was light years away, but they were probably headed for the world the Unseelie used as a staging area.

"Where are the wounded and dead?" I asked.

"I will take you to them, Regent," Ysir said.

I faced Ash and the dragons. "Words can't convey the depth of my gratitude—to all of you. You were staunch and unwavering, the absolute best of allies."

"Come to Fire Mountain as soon as you're able," Ash said.

"Aye, Dariyah's training is far from complete," Goren said.

"Neither is his," Brynn cut in and angled a wingtip my way.

I bowed and said, "We will be there. Meanwhile, let's bend our minds toward a project we'd begun before we were attacked."

"Which one?" Dariyah asked.

"Determining the best way to obliterate the world the Unseelie have been utilizing. I bet it's where the King of Winter took Oberon."

"I have a few ideas to address that," Ysir said. "Give me a day to consult my materials, and I will pull something together."

"We can assist." Ash narrowed his eyes and pointed at two of his contingent. "You shall remain. Let me know if you require aught from Fire Mountain's assets."

The dragons—a red and a gold—nodded understanding. The others built a portal and trudged through it, heading home.

Next, I faced Faery. "Many thanks, my lady."

"None needed. Splitting that Shadow bastard into bits was exhilarating." She turned and followed the path the dragons had carved, using the gateway they'd left open and pulling it shut behind her.

Five of us and the two dragons stood in front of the ruined castle. As I glanced at ruin all around me, the full weight of war descended on my shoulders. "This is a respite," I cautioned everyone.

"Aye," Auril agreed. "A break, and perhaps not all that long. We must be ready because Medusa will scorch the earth seeking retribution for her fallen son."

"Where might we feed?" one of the dragons asked.

"Come with me." Titania crooked a finger. "I will show you a sheep herd you can tap, but only take what you must."

I swallowed a wince. I'd have told them to gorge themselves, but I wouldn't correct Faery's queen. The rest of us returned to the Midnight Court, courtesy of a spell of Auril's making. Where the glade had been empty a while ago, now it contained both injured and dead. Ulane cantered up. "It's over?"

"For now."

"Thought so. I felt the energy of the land shift when the Unseelie departed, the same way it did all those years ago when they chose to leave Faery."

Dariyah gripped my hand briefly. "Mother and I will tend the injured along with Faery's healers."

"Unicorns have sorted the dead." Ulane's voice held somber notes. 'We are ready to begin lighting pyres, but we were waiting for you."

"How many?" I asked, knowing even a single loss was too much to bear.

"Fifty-six." The unicorn rested his horn on my shoulder for the briefest of moments.

Cursing Oberon for seeding the discontent that had

spawned this nightmare, I walked next to Ulane and prepared a few words to say over the dead.

Auril had said there would be two more battles. Could I do this twice more?

It wasn't a fair question because I'd shepherd my land, my realm, through whatever she faced. For now, I focused on sending the souls of those who'd fallen to the *Dreaming* where they could live on without pain. Once it was done, I'd deal with the next task, and the one after that.

Maybe somewhere along the line, I'd have an opportunity to hold Dariyah in my arms, and we could just be the two of us. Those moments would have to be brief, but I'd treasure them like the gemstones she shed as tears. Each perfect and whole and fulfilling.

"This will be the first pyre," Ulane told me.

Kneeling, I said goodbye to men, women, and animals who'd given their lives in Faery's service. Ulane lit the fire, and we moved on.

## CHAPTER SEVENTEEN, DARIYAH

**M**idnight's purring woke me. Or maybe the cat had shifted position. My wings were a total hit with him. He loved snuggling into their feathers. Groggy from too much magic and too much death, my eyes still felt gritty, and my body could have done time on a rack. Hundreds of tiny—and not so tiny—cut places stung and burned; the reservoir that holds my power wasn't fully recovered, either. It hurt in different, non-physical ways that manifested as a creepy sensation something wasn't quite right.

Cyn and I had fallen asleep on the carpet in my flat using wadded up clothing for pillows. I didn't actually remember the magic that brought us here, or how long ago we'd arrived. Maybe a bed would be a sound investment. I had sheets and a cozy duvet tucked away in a closet.

As wiped out as I'd been, I could have zonked out on a bed of nails, but a real bed would be welcome.

Cyn had a house somewhere in Reno, but I hadn't wanted to move Midnight to yet one more new-to-him location. And so, we'd ended up here. Too tired to even stop by the casino for a meal, we'd been in full agreement food could wait. Daylight filtered around the cheap drapes, and I took a moment to assess Cynwrigg's drawn features. It would take more than a few hours of sleep for us to recover. Maybe we never would. Not completely.

My scrappy street fights hadn't marked me like this war did. Not even close. And before this battle, Cyn had been more of an in-name-only regent than anything else. My heart hurt for the mages and animals who'd died. Our losses paled in comparison with the Unseelie, but I didn't care about them. They'd started all this, and—

Except they hadn't. Not really. Oberon had been a driving force, perhaps *the* driving force behind events that had culminated in the war Mother had foreseen all those years ago. If I were honest and took a few steps backward, the loss of anything magical worked against us. Even Father, wicked as he was, had provided a balance point. With him out of the way, Granny would wreak havoc that could have been avoided.

If I'd had a clue how things would shake out, I'd have tried harder to hurt her on that Aegean island of hers. Magic—white and dark—were designed to coexist. This was my first run-in with Shadow Lords or Gorgons or Pegasus, for that matter. If I'd known he was my father, would I have sought him out?

I dug deep, hoping for an honest answer, not pretty words to make me feel better. When I'd been very young, I'd have dropped everything to hunt him down. As I grew, wisdom tempered brashness. I'd have given the matter some hard thought, researched the winged horse before plopping myself on his doorstep and announcing he had spawn he knew nothing about.

Driven by curiosity and a need to tack down the other side of my bloodlines, I would have paid him at least one visit. It would have been a mistake, which might be yet one more reason Mother never let on who he was. Even absent the horse's alliance with the Unseelie king, offering up something he could use against me wasn't wise. Of course, I'd had no idea how wicked he was. Even if I'd investigated him, would I have believed what I found? Or Mother's explanations about how X was related to Y and Z and Q?

I turned my attention to Cynwrigg. We'd showered before falling on our faces last night, so at least we were clean. His high forehead was relaxed in sleep, but once he woke, lines would etch into it and around the corners of his eyes. Neither of us carried our glamour. Our magic would recover quicker without a constant drain.

His long hair had tangled, thanks to falling asleep with it wet. Mine wasn't in any better shape. I cherished the moments we had, but we couldn't tarry. As soon as he woke, we needed to be on our way. Breakfast from Starbucks was quickest, and then we'd teleport to the Midnight Court and check on everyone.

The cat was cradled between one of my wings and a shoulder. I stroked his knotted fur. Maybe I should get him another sack of kitty chow before we left.

I felt Cyn's gaze on me. "You're up," he murmured. "Did you sleep well?"

"Passed out was more like it." I rolled my eyes.

He drew me against him and pressed his lips against my forehead. "If I had my way, we'd go somewhere and block out everything and everyone—except Midnight, of course."

"It's a lovely thought. Maybe someday, but not now."

"I know." He tightened his hold on me before letting go.

Afraid if I didn't get up I'd never leave, I rolled to my feet and got a glass of water from the kitchen sink. Once I'd drained it, I refilled it, padded back across the floor, and offered it to Cyn.

He'd moved to a cross-legged sit. Accepting the glass from me, he drank. "I need clothes," he said. "Give me a few minutes, and I'll be back. Then we'll find something to eat and join the others."

"How are you doing?" I asked and hunkered across from him.

"All right so long as I don't look back or too far ahead. I feel like I failed Faery by not being more on top of things." He shrugged. "Eh. Self-indulgent tripe. I managed Faery as well as I could absent a link with the land. Speaking of which, I am uber relieved she ended up on our side."

"Did you believe the Shadow Lords about her inviting them?"

"I'm not sure what to believe," he replied. "Neither do I think it matters. She threw her lot in with us, and we'll take it and run with it. When she ripped that Shadow Lord to streamers in front of us, she was higher than a kite. I've never seen her like that."

"Guilt can be a harsh mistress," I mumbled. "Any idea what kind of respite we'll have?"

"None, except I bet it won't be very long, and I'm okay with that. I'd just as soon get this behind us. All of it. The piecemeal part is disturbing."

"Know what you mean." I nodded. "If we don't play our hand exactly right, we could still end up with zeroes."

He grinned. "That's right. You're quite the card

shark. I still remember when you had my poor dealer in thrall."

"The casino was a selling point when I signed up with Oberon to spy on you," I admitted.

"If we ever get to the end of this, you can game your heart out. Back soon." Rising to his feet, Cyn shimmered to motes of light.

Midnight meowed loudly. The cat wasn't fond of magical displays, even if he wasn't included in them. I dug clean clothes out of a drawer and got dressed. Once I was done, I checked the state of Midnight's food. He actually had enough, so I filled a couple of bins with kibble.

Cyn popped into the living room wearing dark pants, a pale-blue shirt, and a black jacket. "Ready to go?" he asked.

"Almost."

I walked to him and folded my arms around him. "We'll get through this. One way or another."

He hugged me back. "We will, and then we'll have years ahead of us. An indeterminate number of them."

"Maybe by then I'll know my true name."

"Why does that bother you?" He tipped my chin until our gazes locked.

"Not sure. Everyone else knows theirs, but that makes me sound like a whiny ten-year-old." I licked at my cracked and broken lips. "I was glad not to know it when Pegasus tried to pry it out of me. If he'd had access to it, he probably would have done far worse than he did. Maybe something Ash couldn't have undone."

"I'm not so certain of that," Cyn said. "The mages he held onto were malnourished, but other than that he hadn't harmed them."

"They weren't his blood," I pointed out. "Thanks to an unlikely cavalcade of circumstances, Pegasus caught hell from his primary ally for something he had no idea he'd even done."

"Your mother knew," Cyn said in a studiedly neutral tone.

"She did, but whether she saw them signing on as allies is an open question."

"You could ask her."

"I could, but I'm not going to. It's kind of like with Faery. She made the right choice in the end. What led up to it doesn't really matter." I sucked in a breath and blew it out. "Auril was a good mother. I can't fault her for that. If she picked shit-for-brains mates—or mate since Daddy was a one-night stand—it happened in a different era."

"The Unseelie used to be part of Faery," Cyn reminded me and herded me out the door. We hurried to the corner Starbucks for coffee, sandwiches, and pastries to go. Once we had everything, we melted into an alleyway, and Cyn moved us to the stairway under Lady Luck.

"Do you need to check anything here?" I asked around a mouthful of ham and egg croissant.

"Probably, but I'm not going to. We've been gone too long as it is."

As we strode along, eating and sipping French roast, the barrier to Faery came and went. It didn't prickle as badly as it once had, or perhaps I'd grown used to it.

A quick turn led to the glade of the Midnight Court. It teemed with people, and a cheer rose when we appeared. It made me feel like an imposter. Their cheers were for Cyn, their regent. Not for me. Until I heard both our names.

"Why me?" I asked softly.

"Because you're part of Faery, and part of me," Cyn explained.

We reached Mother's altar and set down our bags and cups. Once our arms were empty, Cyn pulled me close and kissed me. The whoops rose in volume. Had I finally come home?

I almost didn't dare relax into believing such a thing. Every time I'd gotten comfortable since I left Mother's world, it had been snatched away. My go-to place was non-attachment, so I couldn't be hurt when things went south.

*Too late for that,* my wise inner maven observed. *You're already in up to your eyeballs.*

I chuckled.

"What's so funny?" Cyn asked near my ear.

"Nothing. Everything. Let's get this choo-choo chugging down the track. The sooner things are shipshape here, the sooner we can head for Fire Mountain."

"I like a woman with priorities—so long as I'm one of them." He grinned.

I smiled back. "You know you are."


YOU'VE REACHED THE END OF *COURT OF THE FALLEN.* Read on for a snippet from *Court of Destiny*, last of the Magick and Misfits books. While *Court of the Fallen* is fresh in your mind, please leave a review. They mean so much to authors. Doesn't have to be fancy. A sentence or two would be great so other readers just like you can discover what you loved about this series.

Keep reading for a glance into *Court of Destiny*.

# BOOK DESCRIPTION: COURT OF DESTINY

**Urban fantasy and slow burn romance wrapped into a serial that will keep you up reading long into the night.**

**Strange bedfellows rock worlds.**

Faery's castle lies in ruins, a reflection of the rest of a land I love. My land, my realm, has altered almost beyond recognition. The part that hasn't changed is the incredible people and creatures who live in Faery. Unicorns. Fauns. Satyrs. Fae. Sidhe. To name but a few. Their spirits have been indomitable, and it makes me proud to call them brothers.

But then, the Unseelie used to be brethren too. Now

they stand against us along with a collection of monsters intent on sucking every last breath of life from Faery.

The worst part about all of this has been not knowing whom I can call friend. Faery, the incarnation of the land that bears her name, recovered her body, but I don't trust her. Our lead seer confessed her visions have been tainted. We are in the thick of things. As we lurch into the endgame, my life, soul, and fortunes are linked with the woman I love. We rise—or fall—together.

If it comes down to a gut-wrenching choice, will I pick Faery or Dariyah?

## COURT OF DESTINY, CHAPTER ONE, AURIL

Her travel spell took forever. It meant she'd waited nearly too long to return to the world where she'd lived for so many years. First with Dariyah, but then alone. The alone part had been both blessing and curse. She'd always treasured solitude, but the absence of anyone to talk with had worn on her.

"Eh, nothing is perfect," she murmured as the familiar flower scents of her previous home closed around her. She kicked open her magical well and sucked power like a starving child in a famine-ravaged country. Sinking into a crouch, she waited for a modicum of normalcy to return.

This world, this place, would never have sustained her and Dariyah if she hadn't married her magic with it.

At first, the land had appeared suspicious because it steadfastly refused to communicate with her. Back then, she and her toddler had been on the run almost since she'd birthed the child.

She'd been tired and out of options. Or so she'd told herself. The tired part had been true, but surely there'd have been more alternatives if she'd gotten off her ass and looked for them. The kicker, though, had been her daughter gazing at her through the trusting eyes of the very young and begging to stay.

Auril understood why. Out of all the places they'd landed, this one was by far and away the most habitable. Not too warm, not too cold, with lush vegetation, rolling lands, and babbling brooks. So many spots they'd stopped had been freezing or boiling or barely had breathable air.

And so, she'd made this work, but there had been tradeoffs—serious ones. She had to have a method to replenish her power, and the only way it would happen here was if she loaned a good big bunch of herself to the land in return for tapping into its core.

Eventually, they'd developed a balance—all without exchanging a word. The cost had all been on her side. She'd forbidden the land to drain so much as an angstrom of magic from Dariyah. In the absence of any kind of compact, she'd assumed she'd have a battle on her hands one day. It never happened.

The world was content to draw from her and leave her daughter alone. Auril had a hunch it had to do with Pegasus's blood. Evil made most entities with pure magic nervous, and this world might fall into that category.

Her ragged breathing eased as power coursed through her. She'd assumed once she returned to Faery, she'd trade what she'd received on this world for Faery's nourishment. It could still happen, but for now she'd made enough alterations in the fiber and weave of her magic, it no longer matched up with what she could glean from Faery.

Perhaps the spot Dariyah had labelled the *in-between* might work. It restocked her daughter's power, so it might work for her. If her stores hadn't been perilously low, she'd have tried it first. The only problem with that was she'd have to ask Dariyah where it was, which would reveal her problem. Everyone had enough on their plates. She wasn't keen on adding to Dariyah's worries. Not after a series of revelations that had shaken her daughter—and infuriated her too.

Auril set her mouth in a tight line. Decisions she'd made had taken a toll on everyone. She'd known a day would come when she'd have to come clean, but the admission about Dariyah's father was the toughest conversation she'd ever had. She couldn't have released the truth any sooner; it would have placed Dariyah at grave risk. What her daughter didn't know couldn't be wrested from her by force.

If Auril had her way, she'd never have loosed the truth, but events had caught up with her—just as she'd known they would. Seer ability could be a bitch; it shone light into twisted, unpleasant realities. Still refueling her power, she allowed herself the luxury of dipping her toes in the pity pool before snapping out of her sour mood.

After rising from a crouch, she made her way to a cavern with an underground lake. It wasn't her favorite scrying location, but it was the strongest one by far. At least she wasn't swaying on her feet any longer. Neither was she teetering on the edge of falling on her face.

A humming vibrated in the pit of her stomach as she bent to enter the cave. Much like the cavern beneath Faery, this one was studded with crystals embedded in its rock walls. The floor was damp and sandy, and the gentle lapping of water indicated the lake was quiescent.

It could get quite active when she was in the midst of a vision.

Auril clenched her teeth and paced in a circle. Visions. How could hers have been so far off-base? She'd seen Dariyah fighting Pegasus in an aerial battle. It was why her daughter's wings had finally revealed themselves. To challenge her father to a lethal contest. Except it hadn't rolled out that way. Not even close.

Pegasus had captured Dariyah. While shackled by his

power, she'd managed to free his prisoners, but if help hadn't arrived, she'd never have reunited her astral and physical selves. Eventually, she'd have faded to naught but spirit, stuck on a faraway world.

"Maybe I'm underestimating her." Auril continued to talk out loud.

Still, if she'd understood correctly, the only thing that saved Dariyah had been a dragon's quick thinking. Ash had liberated the tiny bit of her essence trapped within Pegasus's magical weave. Being reunited with her missing magic had allowed Dariyah's astral and physical selves to become whole again.

Pegasus was dead—or he should be. Set upon and eaten by the mages he'd imprisoned should have done the trick, but immortality could be tricky. The lead dragon, Ash, had carved out the horse's magical center, but even that could be reversed. It all depended how quickly Medusa and the Gorgon sisters had arrived at Pegasus's lair.

Auril closed her teeth over her lower lip. A far more relevant question was how many of the other events she'd seen had been bogus? And why? Was it a corollary of her long stint on this world? Had it warped her ability to birth true-seeing? The whys didn't matter, though. What did was how much of what she'd imparted to her compatriots back on Faery had been false?

They counted on her, based their strategy decisions

on her information. If everything she'd told them couldn't be counted on, it was miraculous they'd won the last battle. In the future, she'd insist on corroboration from the dragons' seers before promulgating any of her visions as gospel.

And then, there was Danu, her goddess mother. Bitter words had fallen between them. Worse than bitter. Harsh. Angry. Unforgiveable. Auril hadn't sought out Danu for millennia, but neither had her mother reached out to her. As an exceptionally last resort—if it seemed the war was all but lost—she'd choke on humble pie and find Danu. She'd beg, grovel, even apologize, if it brought divine assistance to their cause.

It might not matter what she did. Danu could laugh in her face, spit invectives, and walk away. But at least Auril would have tried.

Wrenching her attention back to her scrying lake, she growled, "Talk to me," sending the words deep into the earth beneath her feet. Usually, she knelt near the lake, but she was too keyed up to sit in one spot. Auril wasn't expecting an answer. This world was stubborn and silent. Perhaps it was incapable of speech, but they could trade imagery. Hell, there were many paths they could have settled upon, but the stumbling block was this world. It wasn't interested in talking to her.

Time slithered past as she scribed a circle so many times she wore a path in the soft sandy dirt. Finally, she forced herself to walk toward her usual spot. Something about it drew her, except today the pull felt stronger than usual. Odd. Nothing about the cave—or this world —had changed.

Why was the combination of lake and sand almost crooning to her?

She stopped in her tracks, no easy task since her feet had developed a will of their own and kicked out as they did their damnedest to propel her body to the place she'd sat hundreds of times.

Perhaps thousands.

"I don't trust you," she said, inserting spaces between each word.

Her right foot quivered with the effort of holding it immobile. The energy swirling around her developed an even more compelling veneer. She'd never fought it before, but then it had never felt so...unnatural.

The flow of power, which had been robust, was drying up. She slammed the gates of her reservoir just in case. Like any tank, its levels were a two-way affair. What flowed in could flow back out just as readily if the source decided she wasn't worthy.

Harsh laughter rolled from her as she hustled out of the cave. The magic endemic to this world was stronger in there than anywhere else. It was why she'd selected that spot for much of her scrying.

She sucked in a breath, blew it out, and did it a few

more times to center herself. She'd lived here hundreds of years. Why had she never questioned the integrity of this world?

"Because it never gave me a reason to doubt it," she answered her own query. Beyond that, most worlds were neutral, benign. This one probably was too, except she'd misread its motives. She'd been convinced sharing her magic was what it wanted.

Sort of a mutually beneficial arrangement. She scratched its back, and in return it fueled her visions and kept her power up to snuff. Waves of invitation wafted from the cave. All she had to do was go back in, take up residence in her usual spot, and all would be well.

The land appreciated her, missed her, wanted everything to fall back into a pattern it had come to value, and—

"Stop!" Auril sliced a hand downward. "You lied to me, manipulated me. You and I are done."

*"You only believe we are. You are mine,"* skittered through her mind.

Auril's eyes widened. She fell back a pace before recovering herself. "I am no one's but my own," she retorted hoping she'd struck a sufficiently assertive note.

Malevolent laughter rose all around her. Rocks cascaded from a nearby cliff. She executed a sideways leap to avoid being struck. Conversation wouldn't buy her anything, so she hurried to the cottage she'd constructed with a combination of her power and what she'd borrowed from the land.

Booms and crashes suggested the land had just withdrawn its contribution to her home. She broke into a run. She'd left things inside, scrolls and scrying implements she'd recover no matter how much rubble buried them.

"If I'm yours," she shouted, "you're treating me quite shabbily."

The land didn't answer. Big surprise since today's words were the first she'd heard in all the centuries she'd called this place home. The usual illusory curtain separating her cottage from plain view was still in place. She swept it aside with a thought and spit curses as the ruins of a dwelling she'd built with determination and sweat equity came into view.

One side had caved in, and the other was working on it thanks to earthquakes shaking it off its foundation stones. Auril didn't hesitate. If she gave away her position, the next part of the cottage would collapse right over her head. She hated to waste her newly resurrected magic, but she funneled some of it into a ward, hoping to buy herself a few minutes.

Everything she wanted to salvage was in one spot. For once, her penchant for organization was paying off.

Banking on stealth, she zigzagged, avoiding obstacles where she could and crawling over others. The cabinet holding her valuables was untouched. Wrapping the whole thing in a transport spell, she moved it out of harm's way, and herself along with it. All around her, the earth boomed and heaved; cracks extended outward in all directions, and the cottage dropped into a sinkhole.

Because she was working against the world, everything required an obscene amount of magic, but it couldn't be helped. She'd always prided herself on her ability to pivot with ever-changing circumstances, but she was rusty. The war provided challenges, but nothing like when she'd been on the run with her baby. Staying out of harm's way had meant no one could find her. If they had, they'd have put two and two together, snatched Dariyah, and tried to do away with the mixed blood mage.

Auril would have fought to the death to keep it from happening. No matter who her adversaries turned out to be, the results wouldn't have been pretty. She hadn't had a leg to stand on, and she'd known it down to her bones. No moral high ground. Nope. That would have belonged to whomever carried out Faery's laws.

"Let it go," she instructed in sharp tones and riffled through the cabinet. If it wouldn't have been such a power hog, she'd have transported the whole thing to save time. A large sack would have been lovely, but she couldn't risk another trip into what had been her home. It sat well below ground level, and she'd run headlong into the world's fury if she risked a second trip.

After tucking items into pockets, she gathered the books and scrolls in her arms. While not as tapped out as when she'd traveled here, the return trip would drain her newly refreshed magic below acceptable levels.

Again.

She'd had to titrate her power all through the last battle. She didn't aim to be in that position a second time. Part of her depletion had occurred pouring power into Dariyah when she'd returned from Pegasus's realm. Auril had done what she had to, not considering how difficult it would be for her to make up the difference.

Ripping and tearing alerted her it was time to go, before the jagged cracks, which were widening by the moment, reached the spot she stood. Would the world stand in her way?

Almost certain the answer was yes, she dropped her warding in favor of tossing everything she had into a journey casting that encompassed her and her possessions. Not that she couldn't have made do without them, but they'd been trusty companions for too long to leave them here. Who knew who might stumble onto this place? She'd found it, which argued others could as well.

The first tenet of magic is believing you can do what you've set out to. Auril visualized the Midnight Court, a place that was more hers than any other, and kindled her casting. Through the space of two long breaths, nothing happened. She was about to goose her casting, heedless of how much magic it took so long as it removed her from what had become a hostile situation.

Turned out, she didn't have to. Where she stood crumpled around her, traded for the familiar dimness of a teleport channel. Breath streamed from her in gasping pants. Her heart was pounding, and she recognized how unnerved she'd been by the specter of spending however long it would have taken for Dariyah to show up.

Her daughter would have figured things out eventually, but Auril hated to be the cause of wasted time, effort, and magic that would have been far better spent fighting to preserve Faery.

At least this visit had unearthed harsh truths, things she should have known—if she'd chosen to look. The only reason she'd been able to draw magic from the world was because of the détente they'd established. An agreement that was no more. Auril still didn't quite understand what she'd done to anger the world to such an extent. Had leaving done it? Or was it when she'd resisted the call to take up her usual scrying seat next to the lake?

Scrunching her tired eyes shut she reconstructed her

visit. Everything had gone along fine until she'd questioned the accuracy of the visions she'd come up with. That was when everything turned to shit. For whatever reason, the world had been skewing her future-seeing.

She didn't believe the world held malevolent intent, or that someone like the Unseelie king was behind any of it. If he'd found her, he'd have rousted her out and done his damnedest to end her. More likely, the world had been alone so long, its way of interacting was overlaying its two cents' worth into her scrying.

She rubbed her eyes before opening them. The motivations of her erstwhile home didn't make a difference. None at all. She had two priorities: figuring out how to add to her magic and letting everyone know her prophecies might have gaping holes in them. Two dragons had remained in Faery, but they weren't seers. She needed to consult with the dragons' blind seers once she'd solved the riddle of how to keep her magic flowing.

The Midnight Court recognized her. Of course, it did. She'd built the place from her essence and her blood. It had kept her from totally running aground magic-wise, but she needed a better solution. Damn. Her thoughts were running in circles. That one had already popped up.

Titrating her magic to the smallest amount needed to keep her spell floating, she held the lore materials close. They were heavy, and her arms full, but she'd be back in Faery soon.

Soon turned out to be on the optimistic side. By the time her journey spell ceded to the glade surrounding the Midnight Court, she was panting with effort. Clearly, moving herself and her possessions hadn't been the swiftest decision, yet she hadn't had a choice.

Everything in her arms clunked onto the ground. She rocked from foot to foot, working on catching her breath and willing a tiny flow of magic from the Midnight Court to salvage her dilapidated energy.

"Sister. Whatever is the matter?" Titania strode to her side and bent to retrieve the lore books. "Ysir will want these for the library he's building."

Several inches shorter than her, Titania was staring speculatively out of golden eyes. With her white hair neatly braided and a fresh robe, she appeared somewhat rested.

"Are you going to tell me? Or not?" Titania pressed.

Complaining went against the grain, so did admitting she might have been wrong. Today was one for doing hard things, though. "It's possible some of my prophecies might not be accurate. We need to check them with the dragon seers' versions."

Drawing her white brows into a single line, Titania said, "And you came up with this how?"

"I returned to the world I spent all that time on."

"And? Come on, Auril, don't make me drag this out of you."

"The short answer is the land and I made a deal. It allowed me to tap magic from its core for Dariyah and me. In return, I shared power with it."

"And then you left." Titania nodded understanding.

Auril blew out a weary breath. She hadn't factored abandonment into the equation. "Aye," she agreed. "I left, and when I returned I harbored doubts about my scrying since Dariyah's battle with Pegasus was so far off the mark."

Titania offered a crooked smile. "Looks like you collected all your toys and left home."

"I did, indeed." Auril swayed on her feet. "I need mead and food and to sit a while. I barely made it back here."

"Faery will replenish your magic." Titania nodded briskly.

With such a strong lead-in, Auril grabbed the bit between her teeth. "You see, there's my second critical problem, or probably my first since everything hinges on it."

"Keep talking," Titania urged.

Her sister's tone had softened, and it wasn't as wrenching as she'd feared to reveal the dilemma around her magic.

*Court of Destiny* will be here before you know it. Releasing toward the end of February 2021, it might, or might not, be the end of this series. We shall see. Meanwhile, you can preorder it wherever e-books are sold.

# ABOUT THE AUTHOR

Ann Gimpel is a USA Today bestselling author. A life-long aficionado of the unusual, she began writing speculative fiction a few years ago. Since then her short fiction has appeared in many webzines and anthologies. Her longer books run the gamut from urban fantasy to paranormal romance. Once upon a time, she nurtured clients. Now she nurtures dark, gritty fantasy stories that push hard against reality. When she's not writing, she's in the backcountry getting down and dirty with her camera. She's published over 85 books to date, with several more planned for 2020 and beyond. A husband, grown children, grandchildren, and wolf hybrids round out her family.

Keep up with her at www.anngimpel.com or http://anngimpel.blogspot.com

If you enjoyed what you read, get in line for special offers and pre-release special reads. Newsletter Signup!

Quinn

Rhiana

Garth

***Coven Enforcers***

Blood and Magic

Blood and Sorcery

Blood and Illusion

***Demon Assassins***

Witch's Bounty

Witch's Bane

Witches Rule

***Dragon Heir***

Dragon's Call

Dragon's Blood

Dragon's Heir

***Dragon Lore***

Highland Secrets

To Love a Highland Dragon

Dragon Maid

Dragon's Dare

Dragon Fury

***Earth Reclaimed***

Earth's Requiem

Earth's Blood

Earth's Hope

***Elemental Witch***

Timespell

Time's Curse

Time's Hostage

***Gatekeeper***

Shadow Reaper

Rebel Reaper

Untamed Reaper

***GenTech Rebellion***

Winning Glory

Honor Bound

Claiming Charity

Loving Hope

Keeping Faith

***Ice Dragon***

Feral Ice

Cursed Ice

Primal Ice

**Magick and Misfits (Fall and Winter 2020)**

Court of Rogues

Midnight Court

Court of the Fallen

Court of Destiny

**Rubicon International**

Garen

Lars

**Soul Dance**

Tarnished Beginnings

Tarnished Legacy

Tarnished Prophecy

Tarnished Journey

**Soul Storm**

Dark Prophecy

Dark Pursuit

Dark Promise

**Underground Heat**

Roman's Gold

Wolf Born

Blood Bond

**Wolf Clan Shifters**

Alice's Alphas

Megan's Mates

Sophie's Shifters

*Wylde Magick*

Gemstone

Lion's Lair

Unbalanced

## STANDALONE BOOKS

Branded, That Old Black Magic Romance (paranormal romance)

Edge of Night (short story collection, paranormal and horror)

Grit is a 4-Letter Word (nonfiction)

Heart's Flame (post-apocalyptic romance)

Icy Passage (science fiction romance)

Marked by Fortune (post-apocalyptic coming of age story)

Melis's Gambit (historical paranormal romance)

Midnight Magic (paranormal romance)

Red Dawn (post-apocalyptic paranormal romance)

Shadow Play (historical paranormal romance)

Shadows in Time (Highland time travel romance)

Since We Fell (contemporary romance)

Warin's War (paranormal romance)